That impossible prettiness of Madelyn's seemed to infuse everything, even the dusk settling around her shoulders like a shawl.

That deep gold thread inside him pulled tight.

That longing in him was something more like a roar.

"Listen to me," she bit out, and whatever he might have been about to do disappeared, lost somewhere in the way she held her hands on her hips, her censorious gray eyes fixed on him. "This will not happen. Troy is not a toy for you to play with. And I am not going to marry you. You might not remember what happened between us, but I do. Just as I remember exactly what was required to survive it. While caring for the child you didn't know existed until yesterday."

He didn't think she should remind him of that part. It wasn't wise. There was still that boiling well of fury inside him, and he didn't see it dissipating any time soon.

But this was not the time for fury. Not directed at his future queen, at any rate.

"You will marry me," he corrected her, without any heat.

USA TODAY bestselling, RITA®-nominated and critically-acclaimed author **Caitlin Crews** has written more than a hundred and thirty books and counting. She has a master's and PhD in English literature, thinks everyone should read more category romance and is always available to discuss her beloved alpha heroes. Just ask. She lives in the Pacific Northwest with her comic book–artist husband, is always planning her next trip and will never, ever, read all the books in her to-be-read pile. Thank goodness.

Books by Caitlin Crews

Harlequin Presents

The Bride He Stole for Christmas
Willed to Wed Him

The Outrageous Accardi Brothers

The Christmas He Claimed the Secretary
The Accidental Accardi Heir

Pregnant Princesses

The Scandal That Made Her His Queen

The Lost Princess Scandal

Crowning His Lost Princess
Reclaiming His Ruined Princess

Visit the Author Profile page
at Harlequin.com for more titles.

Caitlin Crews

A SECRET HEIR TO SECURE HIS THRONE

HARLEQUIN
PRESENTS

H HARLEQUIN®
PRESENTS™

Recycling programs for this product may not exist in your area.

ISBN-13: 978-1-335-73919-3

A Secret Heir to Secure His Throne

Copyright © 2023 by Caitlin Crews

For questions and comments about the quality of this book, please contact us at CustomerService@Harlequin.com.

Harlequin Enterprises ULC
22 Adelaide St. West, 41st Floor
Toronto, Ontario M5H 4E3, Canada
www.Harlequin.com

Printed in U.S.A.

A SECRET HEIR TO SECURE HIS THRONE

CHAPTER ONE

As walks of shame went, this one bordered on epic.

And better yet, gave Madelyn Jones a lot of time to think about the consequences of her foolish actions during her semester abroad back in college. As if she hadn't already spent the past six years doing exactly that.

At some points, hourly.

Though she had thought about it less and less as the years went by. That was what reality did— it chipped away at all the flights of fancy and *what ifs*, not to mention all the pointless angst that went along with it, and what was left was life itself. No more and no less.

Madelyn *liked* her life these days. She'd worked hard to assemble it.

Now it was as if she might as well not have bothered.

She laughed a little at that, though not because it was funny. She was sitting in the back of an armored SUV, halfway up the side of a mountain in the remotest region of the island kingdom of Ilonia, known for winning wars against the Visigoths in antiquity and for otherwise being a largely isolated wet and gray archipelago located off the coast of the Iberian Peninsula, north and east of the Azores.

When a person thought about *island kingdoms*, they thought of sparkling blue waters the temperature of a cozy hug. Or Madelyn did. White-sand beaches beneath graceful palm trees, cocktails festooned with ripe and exotic fruits, and lovely, temperate winters bursting with tropical flowers in a riot of bright colors.

It was just Madelyn's luck that even that was denied her. The capital of Ilonia was on a different island than this one, with an old harbor, colorful buildings arranged prettily enough, and the Royal Ilonian Palace set on the highest hill. That was where they'd landed, and while it was hardly the Caribbean she'd never set foot in but had dreamed about through many a snowy winter, she'd thought it was nice enough. But *this* island—accessible only by one designated and highly regulated ferry or the monarch's personal air transport—was considered the royal refuge in these green and cloudy mountains sticking up out of the Atlantic, covered in deep jungles, volcanic craters, and an improbable number of blue hydrangeas.

Here stood the tallest mountain in Ilonia, Madelyn had been told. With more pride than someone who lived in the American West and knew from tall mountains found reasonable. What that meant in practical terms was that they were high up and it was cold. It was still temperate enough compared to Madelyn's home back in a little village near Lake Tahoe—a vast and mostly unspoiled lake nestled between California and Nevada and currently blanketed by the latest snowstorm, the way it would likely continue to be until June—but still. The slap of the cold as they'd climbed up the winding mountain road—the center vehicle in a convoy, flanked by the Royal Guard—was unexpected.

Like all the rest of what was happening to her.

"You have been cleared to approach the Hermitage, Miss Jones," the forbiddingly sleek older woman beside her said in her smoothly accented English.

For the second time, since Madelyn had yet to make a move.

Madelyn had already gotten all the arguments out of her system. Or, more accurately, she'd grudgingly accepted their futility.

"Lucky me," she murmured, sarcastically, because maybe she was still more in the *grudging* part of her acceptance of this shocking turn her life had taken.

The woman beside her—the terrifying Angelique Silvestri, whose silver hair seemed to gleam with malice—only smiled.

It was the same smile she'd aimed at Madelyn when she presented herself at the front door of the house Madelyn shared with her aunt Corrine, a black-clad entourage splayed out behind her. The same smile that stayed in place throughout each and every interaction that had led them here, across the world and up the side of a mountain in the rain and sleet.

"You agreed to this course of action," the older woman reminded her calmly.

Always so very calmly, as if that made it better.

"It was less an agreement and more blackmail," Madelyn reminded her. She had fought too hard the past six years to take anything lying down. But then she sighed because she also wasn't quite so foolish these days. She didn't take pointless stands that might negatively impact her survival. That wasn't an option available to her. Again, that was reality. That was life. And usually, she thought that was a good thing. "But I'm here. How many people would you estimate have died by slipping off that tiny path and falling to their deaths far below?"

Angelique Silvestri was an Ilonian minister. Madelyn didn't know or care of what.

But she was very good at infusing her every utterance with the weight of her mysterious office when she spoke. "Very few commoners are permitted to set foot on this island, Miss Jones. Those who do are sufficiently aware of the privilege and do not tend to waste the opportunity on histrionics. All you need to do is walk up the path and enter the Hermitage. I hope that's not too much to ask of a girl with your apparent *resourcefulness*."

Madelyn did not dignify that comment with a

response. One of Angelique Silvestri's talents was making it clear that she was delivering a stinging set down, but opaquely enough to leave it open to interpretation. Was she referring to Madelyn's job as a waitress in one of Tahoe's fancier resorts? Or did she mean the fact that Madelyn had never asked for help—or anything else? All that was clear was that *resourcefulness* was not being mentioned as a positive. Not along with the reminder that Madelyn was *a commoner*.

But she bit her tongue because there was nothing to gain by getting into this again. She'd flown all the way here. She'd agreed to this back in Tahoe. There was no point in backing out now just because it was all a little bit more frightening than advertised.

That could be the title of her autobiography, really.

Spurred on by that notion, she pushed open the heavy SUV door—made heavier by the gusting wind and the sleet turned to hail that pelted her. She climbed out, taking a moment to pull the hood of her jacket over her head. It wasn't much help, but she told herself it was better than nothing.

"Sometimes that's all you get," she reminded herself beneath her breath.

Life was nothing if not an opportunity to gather up the lemons and make lemonade.

She didn't look back at the SUV and Angelique, swallowed up behind the tinted windows. Madelyn headed instead for the path up the mountain, which was little more than a narrow hiking trail carved into the forbidding rock. The trail wound away from the small, flat area where the convoy was parked, hugging the steep mountainside as it curved around and headed up.

And up. And up.

Madelyn knew where she was going. She'd dutifully looked at the images while flying over the Atlantic. The Hermitage had been built centuries ago to honor an Ilonian king. It had been carved into the mountain itself and still stood proudly, famous for the lights that beamed out from this otherwise restricted island when a royal was in residence, like a beacon over the archipelago.

Or like the ego of the man she knew waited within.

But there was no point in worrying about *him* just yet, Madelyn told herself. First, there was living through this hike.

The wind picked up as she trudged up the path, doing her best to huddle against the side of the mountain without seeming to do exactly that. She did still have her pride, after all. Pride that was hard-won and well deserved—and she was keenly aware that every step she took drew her closer and closer to one of the major reasons she'd had to fight so hard in the first place.

She didn't like to think about those last few weeks of her study-abroad adventure at Cambridge. Those clear, sunny days that everyone in England had told her were unusual, especially as it wasn't beastly hot, either. The days had been so long. The evenings had stretched on into forever.

And the sweet, warm nights had changed her whole life.

She could still hear his laughter, like it might dance on the wind in this lonely place the way it had seemed to all along the River Cam. She could see all that light and magic sparking in his unusual green eyes, nearly as turquoise as the sea she'd imagined would surround the fanciful island kingdom she'd known—vaguely—he came from.

Just as she could remember how it had ended. Her flight back home had been canceled at the last minute, leaving her with an extra night in England. Instead of staying down in London, she'd taken the train back up to Cambridge. She'd been so thrilled that she would get to surprise him. She'd been so *sure* he would welcome that surprise. She hadn't stopped to think twice. She hadn't stopped or thought at all.

It was cringeworthy, looking back. Madelyn had to take care she didn't cringe herself right off the side of the slick, cold mountain.

Madelyn had hurried into the endless party that was forever going on in the private house where he lived. It sometimes appeared to be a communal-living situation with his friends and sometimes seemed to be only his—he had waved a hand and changed the subject whenever it was raised—but in either case, she had pushed her way through the usual throngs of people and darted up the stairs, bursting with excitement.

But those guards of his that she'd come to consider friends barred her way.

Worse, they'd looked at her with pity. And hadn't let her into his rooms.

And she'd known full well, by then, that there was only ever one reason they kept the Prince from his adoring friends and fans. It was still embarrassing, even now as she tracked up the side of this endless mountain, to remember how long it had taken for the penny to drop. How humiliatingly long she'd *stood* there, staring up at his guards in disbelief because they had always been so friendly to her before and what could possibly have changed...?

"Idiot," she muttered to herself now, picking up her pace on the narrow path. "Complete and utter *fool*."

She told herself the good thing about remembering all the actual details she usually preferred to gloss over these days was that she wasn't tempted to look off the side of the path or imagine, in dizzying detail, exactly what would happen to her if she slipped...

Better to think of that first, perhaps more painful fall, back in Cambridge.

In the present, Madelyn blew out a breath. Back then, she'd turned away from those great doors and his pitying guards. Eventually. But that hadn't been an improvement, because one of his slinky friends waited there, at the top of the stairs. Very much as if she'd gone out of her way to follow Madelyn up from the crowded lounge.

In the aftermath, Madelyn had returned to that moment again and again, and she could only conclude that Annabel—who was Lady Something-or-other-unutterably-posh, yet spent the bulk of her time partying with her family's money—had almost certainly seen Madelyn enter the house. And had followed her up the stairs to take pleasure in what she would find here.

But that night, Annabel had pretended to be sympathetic.

With the same insincerity she'd used while pretending to be friendly over those last few weeks.

Darling, Annabel had purred. *You look positively* crestfallen. *I did warn him that you couldn't possibly know how these games are played. But he's careless, you see. He always has been. No one ever dared tell him not to break his toys.*

What was funny, Madelyn thought as she kept marching resolutely uphill, was that for some time after she'd slunk back to spend a terrible night on a shiny terminal floor in Heathrow, she'd imagined that moment between her and the smirking, completely phony Annabel was the worst of it.

When it had only been the beginning.

It was that last thought that calmed her, though she sped up even more. She wanted out of the cold. Out of the pelting hail. She wanted to do what she'd agreed to do, then march herself right back down to the brittle Angelique, express her sympathies that she'd been unsuccessful because she was sure she would be, and head right back to her life.

Like everything else in life, the only way out was through.

The Madelyn who had staggered out of that house in Cambridge, heartsick and bewildered, had been weak. Foolish and silly, just as Annabel had always intimated, and the fact she had to admit that to herself stung. It had been a bitter pill then and it never got any less bitter.

It was just that Madelyn had grown stronger.

She'd had no choice. She'd lost everything she'd thought mattered to her, as surely as if she'd set her life on fire. But it turned out she was a phoenix, because she'd learned how to rise up anyway. These days, she thought of the fire as the thing that had made her, not destroyed her.

And all this was, she thought as she wound around the side of the mountain again and saw that stone-cut building before her in the gloom, was a little bit of leftover ash. Easily enough given over to the wind, then hopefully forgotten.

Madelyn studied the Hermitage as she climbed the last little way. It was even more impressive up close, where she could see that the ancient artisans really had etched the building from the mountain itself. From a distance, it looked as if it floated here, somehow holding the peak up above it while perched so prettily on the bulk of the mountain below. Up close, it was less pretty and more…a kind of shrine to a certain ruthlessness, really.

Because who climbed this far up the side of an inhospitable mountain and thought, *Why, yes. I will fashion myself a dwelling place here and make myself a part of the mountain itself.*

But even as she thought that, something in her knew the answer.

The Hermitage rose several stories above the path, on the other side of a stone arch and an ancient gate that could have guarded the entrance to any medieval keep. As she approached, she looked around, not for a doorbell or anything so modern, but for some kind of ancient device—a bellpull or the like—that might allow her to signal whoever lurked within that she was here.

A part of her hoped there was nothing. Or even if there was, that it would fail to raise the Hermitage's lone inhabitant. She was already plotting out how she would sorrowfully explain to Angelique that there was nothing to be done. That she couldn't even gain entrance, and so it was best all round if she simply took herself back home and let the Kingdom of Ilonia sort itself out without her.

Madelyn felt the most cheerful she'd been in days as the path opened up a bit wider here at the top, to fit in all that stone and drama.

But her hopes were crushed when she got closer

and realized that there was a little door in the great gate, and it already stood open.

Muttering under her breath, Madelyn forced herself to step right on through instead of standing there, thinking better of it.

Inside, she blinked as she looked around, because she was still outside, if beneath the outcropping above. She'd walked into what looked like some kind of castle keep and realized that what she'd taken for an ornate window between one floor and the next was actually a perfect place to pace around, staring down at the world far below. On clear days, Angelique Silvestri's assistant had informed her on the plane, it was possible to see the entire sweep of Ilonia from the hallowed heights of the Hermitage. Madelyn hadn't cared much about that while flying. But now that she was up here, she found herself almost wishing that it was clear today. Because she imagined the view must be spectacular enough to almost make even her forced march worth it.

And that was when some faint little movement in the corner of her eye caught her attention. So she turned her head, and there he was.

Her breath caught.

Seeing him, it turned out, was significantly worse than *imagining seeing him* had been all these years.

Seeing him was like getting torn wide open. She was shocked she withstood the impact of it. She thought she might have crumpled, or screamed, or simply...*imploded.*

But she didn't. She stood fast.

She reminded herself that she had already survived him.

Defiantly, Madelyn took a big, deep breath and told herself it was the melodrama of this situation that was getting to her, nothing more.

There was no need to *feel* anything, she told herself. She eyed him critically instead.

He stood there at the top of the carved stone stairs. He was dressed in black. A pair of black boots that looked better suited to combat, even from a distance. A pair of tactical trousers that rode low on his hips, as if he planned to scale a fortress later on. And a T-shirt that did its job of defining each and every muscle in his upper body far too well.

He had been lean and beautiful when she'd known him. Almost ethereal, as his many admirers had sighed and simpered. His hair had been longer, a mess of blond waves that had made him look like a myth. Today, that hair was close cropped and much darker, giving him the look of a kind of burnished gold and lending him an air of intensity that made her skin seem to tighten where she stood.

But it wasn't his *hair* that was the most disconcerting, she corrected herself. It wasn't all the messy things inside her that she refused to admit she was feeling. It was that he wasn't smiling.

His mouth was set in a hard line, though that didn't diminish the sensuality that had always been one of the first things anyone ever noticed about him—a presence and charisma that could light up whole cities without his even trying—but, rather, made it something else again. He had always seemed amused by his effect on others. He'd appeared entertained by the arrangement of his features, as if he'd had a hand in making himself so beautiful. Those high cheekbones, that mouth, the dazzling symmetry of his objectively perfect face.

Today, there was nothing that suggested entertainment or amusement anywhere in him. He looked... *tougher*, Madelyn thought. Though that was a remarkably strange word to use about this man. A man she always pictured lounging somewhere. A man so languid and committed to his own pleasure that he could make a simple morning stretch, still lying in bed, a symphony of sensuality if he chose.

It was not that this harder, more intense man had lost that sensuality. It was more that it had shifted into a kind of brooding masculinity that seemed to carve its way deep inside Madelyn where she stood. Then it was not only that her skin prickled, but also that she could feel that same tightening wind around and around inside her, spiraling down until she felt it twist into heat at her core.

She shouldn't have been surprised.

This was the problem with this man. This was his sorcery. Madelyn had been levelheaded and rational, not at all the sort to have her head turned by the glittering mob of Cambridge's excruciatingly glamorous upper class. She'd worked too hard to get there. She'd known exactly who she was. She'd been proud of her modest beginnings, her down-to-earth upbringing. Her goal in life had been to make her parents proud, then do something worthwhile with her life to prove that she was worth all the education neither Angie nor Timothy Jones had ever thought was worth the bother.

Instead, one night she'd walked into the wrong pub—filled, for some reason, with a collection of bright and shining young things who the friends she'd been with had informed her spent most of their days on the pages of *Tatler*. When not yacht-hopping across the Mediterranean or sequestering themselves on breathtakingly posh estates from Vanuatu to Positano and back again.

Madelyn had glanced their way with the sort of interest she might have shown a cage of sleeping creatures in a zoo.

But he'd looked back. Their eyes had met, then held.

And nothing had ever been the same.

She'd found a prince in England, just as her friends back home had teased her she would. Sadly for her, he'd used his charm to talk her into behavior that was so unlike the staid, prim, studious girl she'd been that she'd spent all the years in between wondering how on earth he'd ever compelled her to do it.

But as he slowly descended those stairs, she found, to her dismay, that she understood the former version of herself entirely.

Even though he wasn't smiling today. Even though his approach seemed far more measured, far less breathless and bright. Even though it was different, he still managed to make her forget that they were stuck together in a heap of stone thousands of feet above the ground. On this island in the middle of nowhere, closer to Iceland than the coast of Portugal. He made her forget everything except him, as if he was still as inevitable as he'd seemed then.

It was the way he walked, as if the entire universe had been created to celebrate every step he took and to arrange itself around him as he moved.

It was the way he focused on her, intent and decisive enough that she had the same stray panic she'd had years ago, wondering if he could read every single thought she had inside her head.

It didn't matter that this version of him seemed grim and changed.

It was still him. Paris Apollo of Ilonia. The man who had altered the entire course of her life.

She stood straighter. She lifted her chin as he stopped before her, there in the half-protected stone yard of this ancient place.

"I will admit that I am intrigued," he said, and it was still his voice. She still recognized it, much as she'd like to deny that, because that recognition was *physical*. It rolled through her like fire, leaving the same scorch marks it always had. "To discover why, having failed to compel me with all of the previous emissaries they've sent to beg and beseech me, they settled on a slip of a woman in cheap shoes."

Madelyn took that in. And did not indulge the spark of outrage deep inside her that wanted to inform him that these were the most expensive shoes she owned. Because there was scrimping and there was saving, and then there was appropriate footwear for life beside Lake Tahoe, where it was always necessary to be ready for any and all weather at any given time.

Because she was certain he knew perfectly well that he was being rude.

"Nothing to say?" His voice was quiet and somehow more…commanding than she recalled. But then, she needed to catch up to current events. Paris Apollo was a king now. He'd been elevated from the Prince she'd known two years ago, when his parents had been killed. "They cannot possibly have sent me a woman for pleasure. If they had, I feel certain they would not have chosen you. Some nameless creature, wan and faintly disapproving. These things do not stir the body or the blood, I think you'll find."

That was even more astonishing, as she assumed it was meant to be. And Madelyn could not say that she cared much for his choice of descriptors, but she couldn't really argue with his assessment, either. "I flew halfway around the world to climb an inhospitable mountain and be insulted by you for the effort. You're lucky I'm not significantly more disheveled."

"I think someone has made yet another error in

judgment." He prowled closer and peered down at her, as if looking for evidence of that error. On her face. "It's not that there isn't something pleasing about your appearance, you understand. A whiff of innocence to go along with the American accent. They should have told you that I have always preferred my lovers to be rather more sophisticated."

And he was already stepping back again, flipping the back of his hand in her direction to dismiss her before she'd processed what he'd said.

Not the fact that he seemed to think she'd been sent in like a royal harlot.

But the other, more critical part.

She tilted her head to one side. And considered a possibility she would have assumed was inconceivable. "You don't know who I am?"

He paused. Considered her. His eyes seemed to gleam. "Should I?"

A thousand possible responses to that flooded her. There was outrage and insult aplenty. She couldn't deny that. And maybe, buried way down beneath it, some kind of hurt, too.

Because she certainly remembered him. Every single day, whether she liked it or not.

But in all of this, it had never occurred to her that he would fail to remember her in turn.

She wasn't sure she believed him. Even so, she wanted to remind him exactly who she was and who she'd been to him, if briefly. So much that she *ached* with all the things she didn't say. She wanted to give him dates and times and even produce the one photograph she had of the two of them together, but she didn't.

Because if he didn't remember her, Madelyn couldn't influence him one way or the other, and that was her entire reason for being here.

And if she couldn't influence him, if she didn't have the leverage on him that Angelique Silvestri had imagined she would, Madelyn might as well turn right around and leave.

There was a different kind of sensation drumming in her then, electric and intense. She told herself it was relief. And that she would do her due diligence, nothing more. "Is this all a lot of smoke and mirrors to cover up a case of royal amnesia?"

Those pale green eyes of his looked even more unworldly set against his darker, shorter hair. She noticed things she didn't remember, like how sooty his lashes were. And he was still as beautiful as ever, but it was all changed now. As if he'd spent all these years since she'd last seen him ridding himself of anything that was soft or accessible or languid until there was nothing left but this...*tempered steel*.

As if he was more a weapon than a king.

"Is that the prevailing propaganda?" he asked softly. "Is it my incapacity they whisper of in the palace? Are you here to bear witness to it? It's an inspired choice, I grant you. You somehow manage to look both as if butter wouldn't melt and yet practical. I can already see you giving reluctant interviews to anyone who asks. Poor Paris Apollo, so diminished. So unequal to his role, as everyone expected after his misspent youth. You have my blessing to tell them whatever you wish."

"So that's a no, then, on the head injury? You're not suffering from any kind of condition—you legitimately don't remember me. You have absolutely no idea who I am."

She tried not to sound as pleased by that as she told herself she felt.

"I've never liked tests," he said, and there was a hint, then, of the amusing, rambling, philosophical way he'd used to talk. So leisurely and unconcerned about everything because, truly, he'd been the most unsuitable Crown Prince anyone in Europe had ever heard of. Or so the tabloids had claimed. "Do you think I ought to recognize you?"

Madelyn felt something enormous inside her... shift.

And as it did, a kind of giddiness flooded in behind it.

She told herself that was what it was.

"No," she said. "Certainly not."

She did not curse his name. She did not indulge the part of her that would always be that foolish girl standing outside his bedroom door, unable to process that he'd moved on before she'd even left the country. Or that, in all likelihood, he'd never considered them a couple at all in the way that she had. She didn't offer proof that she knew him. Because a part of her had long since accepted that in reality, she didn't. She hadn't. She'd never known him, because if she had, her life would look very different than it did now.

And she *liked* her life, she reminded herself. Fiercely. Just as it was now, which didn't mean that it was without difficulty—but it was hers. She'd made it. She claimed it.

It wasn't her fault that his was a disaster, despite or because of his entire government playing games like this one. He clearly had no interest in fixing it, but why should she care? This had nothing to do with her.

"No," she said again, more firmly. "If you don't know me, you don't know me. Enjoy your…hermiting."

And then she turned and headed for the door and the path down the mountain, more than ready to get the hell out of this unpleasant spiral into the past before it ate her whole.

CHAPTER TWO

MADELYN JONES WAS an inspired choice.

Paris Apollo could admit that, little as he liked it.

That Paris Apollo found himself King was a travesty beyond the telling of it. Every morning he woke enraged anew that this terrible thing had come to pass so far ahead of schedule. It had been nearly two entire years since his unwilling ascension, and if anything, his dark fury had only increased. Grief did not improve it. Solitude did not dissipate it.

Instead, it had become a part of him. Like breath. Like blood.

Like the yearning for vengeance that consumed him whole.

But this was not the time to think about his parents' murder. This was not the time to unveil the great reckoning he had spent every moment of his time here planning.

Because the woman his ministers had sent him today—the latest in a long line of attempted lures and obvious bait and any number of attempts to sway him from the ancient, traditional retreat he had insisted upon taking though the world had gone modern—was the last woman he'd ever wish to see.

She was the one who had nearly wrecked him, back when he'd been so determined to live as loud and as wild as he could before his life of duty would begin. She was the one who had very nearly had him turning all his plans for committed debauchery on end...

He had thanked what gods there were, day and night for years, that he'd been saved from that fate by the most unlikely source. That the reality of the situation had been explained to him. That while he was a prince and would one day be a king—and had, it turned out, harbored a secret wish to make himself over into the kind of love story his parents had been—the object of his affection was an American student studying abroad.

She will go home and tell great tales of her escapades in London with a real, live prince, his friend Annabel had told him, and she had been in a position to know. She and Madelyn had become fast friends. *That's what she talks about most when you are not about, Paris Apollo. Do what you like, but are you really going to upend your whole life for a girl who sees you as a little fling best left abroad?*

It served him right, he'd thought, that he'd imagined he could live up to his parents' example. When, deep down, he'd always been certain that he wasn't made like them. That he wasn't good enough to love like that, for a start. He had been sickened by his own sentiment.

Much as he was now sickened by the sybaritic creature he'd once been—and the great many things he'd done to forget about this woman who dared present herself before him again.

That playboy fool disgusted him now, but then again, so did this woman who had led him to fling himself headlong into some of his worst excesses. That was how badly he had taken her leaving him and never looking back. Never even reaching out to him once she'd gone.

Her silence had proved that Annabel had told him nothing but the unpleasant truth.

Paris Apollo had never imagined he would see Madelyn again, and that had suited him fine. He had imagined that she was off having a gleaming little life, telling stories of her glory days. He had made sure *his* glory claimed a prominent place on every tabloid going, lest she imagine for a second that he had even noticed her departure.

He had been halfway to forgetting her before his parents died.

And now he couldn't think of anything that mattered less. But he knew this was not the time for self-loathing—or, rather, any *more* self-loathing than he already indulged in regularly. There were things to be done and a whole lifetime that yawned out before him with ample opportunity to hate himself as he deserved.

"Wait," he ordered her.

Because Paris Apollo could admit that he was faintly intrigued that a woman like her had turned to go in the first place. And it only grew when she didn't stop walking. When she didn't turn to stone or fawn all over herself while awaiting his next instruction.

It was certainly something different. None of the others had left until he'd ordered them away. Some had even required threats to leave the Royal Isle.

She was always something different, a voice in him whispered, but he shoved it aside. She had left him and never looked back. Why was he shocked that this time, she was doing it where he could see it?

"I ordered you to stop," he said, quietly enough, but even he could hear the stark command in his own voice. Once, he might have mourned the change in him. That he should sound not only so unlike himself, but also very much like all of those he had hated and disdained in turn. Or had simply found tiresome when he was young and feckless, like his poor father.

But it worked.

Madelyn turned, though she took her time with it. "You said you don't remember me." She folded her arms, reminding him with that gesture that she really was an American, with no innate understanding of the deference due her betters. The old him might have admired that. Well. He knew all too well that he had. "But to clarify, I'm not one of your subjects. You're not the boss of me. Or anything in between."

He lifted a brow and decided that his knee-jerk decision to pretend he didn't know her was inspired. "Yet you must be something to me or they wouldn't have sent you."

She stiffened as if outraged. When normally women were only too happy to fight for the opportunity to get this close to him. And despite how easily she had left him six years ago, he knew beyond any possible doubt that she had once yearned for him. Ached for him. Hungered for him, body and soul.

Body, he reminded himself darkly. *Her* soul *was never involved—only yours.*

"Tell me, which one of my devious ministers dispatched you up the side of my mountain?" When she only glared back at him, Paris Apollo let his mouth curve. It was not a smile. "Angelique, if I had to guess."

He could tell he'd hit his target by the way Madelyn pressed her lips together.

And he'd been trying to insult her before. He'd had an opportunity to lash out and he'd taken it, and he wanted to assure himself he didn't regret it…when he knew he did. If only because it was as if he had learned nothing at all these last terrible years.

The truth about Madelyn was nothing so simple as *wan*. She was fresh faced and innocent-looking in the quintessentially American fashion, fair enough. But she was also remarkably *pretty*.

God help him, she was still so damned pretty.

And she still lit him up as if the only light in the

whole of the world was her. When he knew it wasn't. Because she had taken it with her when she'd gone, and the sun had still found a way to rise. Summers had waxed on forever. There had been light enough.

But there hadn't been *her,* and he was furious he even noticed. When he wanted, so badly it felt like another betrayal, to be immune to Madelyn Jones at last.

He studied her, trying to reason out *why* she affected him so much. Why she always had. There was the long blond hair and surprising gray eyes. That lean figure, skinny in a way that suggested something other than fashion. Head to toe, she looked... haphazardly put together, as if she'd thrown on the clothes she wore with no thought and spent even less time on her hair.

As if she had actually done this, not spent hours to achieve a certain curated version of carelessness when she was anything but. She was not stunning and sophisticated like most of the women who had cluttered up his orbit before—and after.

She never had been.

Madelyn had been artless and earnest, and God help him, he did not intend to go down that road again. Not when he knew how it ended.

Not when he knew that he had been nothing to her but a spot of *sightseeing.*

And no matter that there was still that same maddening *something* about her that made the memory of other women seem overdone and labored in contrast. As if her inescapable prettiness was not only greater than the sum of her parts, but also a sort of fresh breeze that blew out the cobwebs of all those women who tried too hard for his attention.

It would have been easier, then and now, if she'd merely been beautiful. Beauty was a commodity. *Pretty* was impossible to define and harder still to sell. Yet everyone knew it when they saw it. When they were nearly struck speechless at the sight of it.

More than all that, she looked *kind,* he thought—

And then nearly barked out a bitter laugh at that line of thinking. Because he knew all too well how little kindness there really was in this world, and how seldom it mattered anyway. Or his parents would still be alive.

But this was still not the time to unleash the full force of the darkness inside him.

Not when he already knew, without doubt, that what he thought he saw in her wasn't there. It never had been.

"If you are not here to tempt me," he murmured instead, "as that is not how Angelique operates, why are you here?"

"Why does anybody come all the way up here to see you?" She sniffed with a disdain Paris Apollo had only seen before in films. Never directed at himself. For even at his most dissipated, he had still been *himself.* Who would dare disdain the Crown Prince of Ilonia to his face? And if anyone would, he could not imagine it being *Madelyn*, who had once made him believe he might possibly have hung all the stars. Just for her. "I understand that a great many have been sent. And all have failed. Not that anyone has asked me for my opinion, but if you're *that* interested in remaining in a big stone castle on the top of a little-known mountain, I'd be inclined to let you do it. After all, that's what the world needs, we can all agree. One more outrageously wealthy man on a personal quest that inconveniences as many people as possible."

Something stirred inside Paris Apollo at that, and it took him far too long to identify it.

Laughter.

Actual laughter, not its dark and bitter shadow.

He had the urge to laugh, out loud, and that was disconcerting in the extreme.

Obviously he repressed it. "This is the kingdom of Ilonia," he told her.

"And here I thought I was in London. I did think it seemed a bit more rustic than I remembered."

"You are American, are you not? It is never clear what an American might know of the world."

Her gray eyes gleamed. "One thing Americans are usually pretty clear on is the irrelevance of kings."

Again, that urge to laugh. He remembered that too well. Again, Paris Apollo repressed it. That was new. "It is tradition that when an Ilonian king dies, his successor retreats from public life for a year out of respect. And, if we're being less high-minded, because there is often a great deal of tutoring of the new monarch that everyone prefers remaining unseen by the general public. The same is true when an Ilonian queen dies. Perhaps you are unaware that both the King and Queen died. At once. Therefore, a two-year retreat from public life was the appropriate response, no matter what my ministers might think."

She paused then, looking away from him. "I'm sorry, Paris Apollo. I think it's easy to speak of kings and queens in the abstract, but they were your parents. I can't imagine how you feel."

He steeled himself against the concerning part of him that wanted to believe her. When she was only here as a part of one more political game—one more gambit on the part of his ministers to make him do things their way, not his. "I do not wish you to imagine it. I do not need anyone else to imagine it."

Because he lived it. And he had taken the things he felt and made them stone. Just like the Hermitage here on this mountain, he'd carved that stone to suit his aims.

For Paris Apollo would have his vengeance. He would weed out everyone responsible for his parents' demise, and he would make them pay. By his own hand, if necessary.

"I don't require condolences," he growled when her forehead creased, her gray eyes grew somber, and she seemed inclined to offer a few. "All I wish is to be left alone to conduct the traditional grieving period allocated to every Ilonian monarch in history. It does not seem like too much to ask, and yet here you are. The last in a long line of those who wish to drag me back to the palace, tradition be damned."

Her arms were still folded. Her gray gaze grew... opaque.

Paris Apollo could not understand why that gnawed at him. Why he felt that she should be open, melting, easily read instead—when that girl was as much a construction as any other story he'd ever told himself.

This woman might as well be a stranger. That was why he was treating her like one.

"My understanding is that your two years are up," she said after a moment. "Or about to be up, more accurately. Should you not appear in three days' time, it will trigger a constitutional crisis and your cousin, the Honorable Lord Konos, will take the throne."

As if he had somehow missed that little detail. As if he needed her, imported from her carefree American life, to share these things with him.

He did not choose to focus on that part, lest his temper exceed his control. "There is nothing honorable about Lord Konos."

"I'm not an expert on Ilonian politics and can only repeat what I've been told, but apparently, you are not the only person who thinks King Konos would be a bad idea."

Paris Apollo did not react to that. Not outwardly. For his treacherous, murderous cousin Konos would take that throne over Paris Apollo's dead body.

Something his cousin would no doubt take great

pleasure in producing for the country, but Paris Apollo was ready for Konos and his machinations. He had done nothing these last two years but prepare for the day he would come down from this mountain and clean up the mess Konos had made.

"The throne is not in jeopardy," he said now. "I've told Angelique and all the rest of my ministers this myself. The Hermitage might look ancient, but I assure you, it is sufficiently wired to carry the concerns of my country to my ears at all times of the day and night. Ilonia is not running itself. I am removed from the palace, but I have not abdicated my responsibilities."

Only after he said that did he realize that he… was justifying himself to Madelyn Jones, who had already walked away from him twice. As if he was not the King. As if she had some power over him.

The important thing was that he didn't know why she had been sent here to him. Why should Angelique Silvestri imagine that one of the many women Paris Apollo had sampled in his day might sway him one way or another?

"Terrific," Madelyn replied dryly, her gaze moving over his face in a way he could not say he liked. "Now that we've settled that, I'll just head on back down the mountain, let your friend know, and be on my way."

He was shaking his head before he knew he meant to move, much less betray a reaction.

"I think not," Paris Apollo said, and not because

she was a *pretty light*. But because Angelique was a canny politician who did nothing without a reason, and he didn't want Madelyn wandering off until he figured out what that reason was.

That she still held such power over him was yet one more cross to bear.

Paris Apollo told himself he would ignore it like all the rest.

For her part, Madelyn frowned. "You couldn't wait to be rid of me a few minutes ago. I was far too unsophisticated for your taste. Too beneath you to even rate a conversation. Now, suddenly, you've changed your mind?"

"Kings do not change their minds, but, of course, you wouldn't know that. You are from a country entirely comprised of upstart peasants."

"Thank you for the history lesson." And while the look in her eyes bordered on insolent, she managed to keep her tone perfectly smooth. Unobjectionable. He should not have found it enraging. "Sadly, it looks like the rain and hail is only going to get worse. I expect that the path downhill will be slippery. So I'd better get to it."

"But it doesn't make sense."

He closed the distance between them again and this time walked around her in a circle, studying her. Taking in all the various puzzle pieces that were his life, his dark reign, and everything he knew about his court and his ministers and all the other things that made up the crown he'd never wanted. He turned it this way and that.

"It's impossible that Angelique Silvestri would do anything at random. She's a woman of brutal efficiency."

This blonde American who had once come *this close* to turning his life upside down and inside out… sniffed. "I would have said malice and self-possession."

"That, too, certainly, but you have to consider her end game."

Paris Apollo was beginning to think that Madelyn had truly slept on that hair and hadn't bothered to fix it. And she certainly hadn't fussed with her appearance since she'd arrived. It was as if she wanted him to believe she didn't care one way or another.

He was not sure he could believe she *truly* didn't care.

Or maybe he couldn't bear to think she didn't. That notion twisted in him oddly, so he pushed on. "Angelique wants me off this mountain and back in the palace so she can demonstrate to the whole kingdom that she has the new King's ear, just as she always had my father's. She would not send you here to tempt me or play games. She would send you only if she thought you could convince me to move at her pace rather than mine. But why would she think *you* capable of such a thing?"

Madelyn's eyes narrowed. "I have no earthly idea."

And the thing Paris Apollo still couldn't get past

was that he'd believed he would have more time. His parents had been in excellent health. They should have ruled for decades more. He had quite expected to find himself edging out the record holder for longest reign as a crown prince in Europe since his father had taken the throne three days after his nineteenth birthday and had announced his intention to hold it until he was ninety-nine.

King Aether had been known far and wide as a man of his word.

Paris Apollo had thought he'd had time, and so he'd wasted it. He had not tied himself down to the usual concerns of heirs to thrones. He had consoled himself—or, rather, he had attempted to console his father—by shrugging it all off. Especially in the wake of his brief affair with the one woman he'd taken seriously. He'd reminded Aether that Ilonia was, when all was said and done, a tiny island. With a population smaller than any other kingdom in Europe, and the bulk of them staunch supporters of the monarchy.

You worry too much, he had teased the old man. *There are only so many lives I can ruin with my profligate ways, after all.*

You are less amusing than you think, his father had replied.

But he had laughed.

Because Paris Apollo had been the apple of his parents' eyes. Their pride and joy, for he had come to them late in life and long after it had been widely accepted that his mother would bear no issue.

We were a love match, Queen Neme used to tell him. *And we were content with each other. We had accepted that this particular branch of the bloodline would end with us. But then you proved us wrong, darling boy, as you always do.*

He had assumed his people would forgive him for his behavior, too. Because they always had. Because he was the kingdom's favorite son.

Because they—and he—had been so certain that he would have ample time to have a second act. To grow up. To become the sort of king they deserved, just as his father had before him.

He had not imagined he would ever find a love match. He had not believed he had such emotion within him, though he knew saying so would break his parents' hearts, for they had wanted him to find what they had above all things.

For a few bright weeks—barely two months—six years ago, he had almost thought...

But Madelyn had shown him how foolish he had been to surrender to such fantasies. Love was a lightning strike from on high and he was not likely to get hit. One day, far in the future, he would do his duty as required. As he had always planned he would, without concerning himself with *light* of any sort.

In the meanwhile, he had wasted his time. Aggressively. He understood that too well.

Yet while he'd been out there scandalizing the tutting tabloids, he'd gotten good at reading people in a way he doubted others in his position ever did. Most royals were surrounded by palace aides and courtiers trained to tell them what they wished to hear. Paris Apollo had committed a great many sins. He could not pretend otherwise. But at least he had not lived in an echo chamber.

That was a thin comfort these days, but he knew Madelyn was telling him the truth. That she didn't really know what she was doing here...

Though the more he studied her expression, the more he thought that perhaps that was not *all* of the truth. "You might not believe you need to be here, but I suspect you know why Angelique thinks you ought to be. Is that not so?"

Once again, her gray eyes were impossible to read, and he resented it. He remembered a time when he had known every stray thought that crossed her face.

When he had shared them.

Though it infuriated him that he should view this as a loss. When he had lost so many other things of far greater value than the innocence of a girl he should have forgotten by now.

"I think she thought you would recognize me. Or maybe she only hoped you might." Madelyn shrugged, but he couldn't quite believe her insouciance. Not quite. "Either way, you don't."

"And every time you say that, it becomes all the more clear that I should." And he didn't like how he felt, so he took it out on her. He didn't pretend otherwise. He tilted his head to one side. "Tell me your name."

The way she looked at him then was…mutinous. He saw her nostrils flare as if she was fighting an intense reaction. He watched that glittering thing in her gray gaze, deeper than any mere *temper*.

All he did was wait. He felt the cold wind on his face, the press of the damp. He could smell a new snowstorm coming in, this high up.

But snow wasn't lightning. He would do well to remember that.

Like all the other things he'd forced himself to remember on this mountain. To learn. The silence here was a blaring thing. The elements were teachers, leading him out of his scandalous, wasteful past and into this dark future.

Making him into a weapon.

Making him nothing at all but vengeance.

Until now, Paris Apollo had been grateful for all of these things. He found he resented this woman for awakening all the other parts of him that he'd cast aside when he'd come here, broken and grieving and determined to fix what had happened the only way he could.

"Madelyn," she offered. Eventually. But she didn't sound agreeable or obedient. Her gaze darkened as she glared back at him, as if she resented him right back. As if she dared that, too. She cleared her throat. "Madelyn Jones."

And her name in her own voice rang in him. Like a scrap of a forgotten song. A lyric, maybe, though the melody was lost. Though he told himself he was no singer, and he knew no good could come of recalling that long-ago night in a Cambridge pub, he said, "I know that name."

"My last name is Jones." Her tone was as suspiciously bland as her gaze was a storm cloud. "People do tend to recognize it. What with it being common as dirt and all."

"Was that an attempt to be scathing?" he asked, and then he smiled like it was still two years ago. As if he had nothing to think about but the pursuit of his own pleasure. As if all he was or ever would be was lazy and at his ease, a wastrel through and through. "I should warn you, I'm impossible to shame."

She shifted her weight and he got the distinct impression that he had somehow lived down to her worst expectations of him. The old Paris Apollo would have delighted in it.

Or so he told himself.

When he had a sneaking suspicion that she was the only person still alive that he had ever really wanted to impress.

Maybe a part of him still did.

That notion told him, in no uncertain terms, that it really was time to leave the Hermitage, regardless of any looming power grabs from the likes of Konos. Or the constitutional crises some ministers seemed to imagine he would ever let happen.

"I don't require a personal connection with you to know how shameless you are," Madelyn was saying, which he supposed wasn't a lie. Not quite. "I live in the world, Paris Apollo. Even all the way in the darkest wilds of America, your every exploit has been foisted upon us all since you were born."

"Some people detest their celebrity, particularly when they did not choose it themselves." He studied her closely but still could not seem to find the Madelyn he'd known so well in her face. Only the image of her over the cool gaze of a woman he would have called a stranger. "I have never been one of them."

Another one of her judgmental little sniffs. "I'm not sure that I would brag about that."

"Madelyn Jones. Improbably American, when I have never set foot on that continent. Worryingly dispatched to the Hermitage by Angelique Silvestri herself. The mystery goes deeper and deeper."

"I'm sorry you find this mysterious, though, if I'm honest, I do, too. It wasn't my idea to hunt you down up here. Everyone grieves in their own time, after all."

"Angelique is a master manipulator. If she sent you here, she has a reason."

"That doesn't mean that I know her reason."

"And yet, Madelyn Jones, I think you do." He wanted to reach out and touch her. He refrained. Furiously. "Why don't you tell me what Angelique thinks your presence here will achieve?"

He thought she would fob him off again. Go round and round another circle.

His hand itched as if *not* running his palm over the damp cascade of blond hair before him was a kind of torture.

And watched her as she clearly weighed pros and cons he couldn't name. He could *see* those scales in her gray eyes.

He hated this, too.

"I don't know what she thinks about anything," Madelyn said after a long moment, when the wind picked up and shot around the courtyard, slicing into him as if it was still winter. "She's far too hard to read."

"But…?"

"But." She took a breath, then let it go. And somehow seemed to grow another inch or two as she stood there, gazing back at him. "Well. It's about Troy."

"Troy," he repeated flatly. Disappointed that she was continuing to play games. "The myth? Should I view you as the personification of the Trojan horse? Is that why you came here—to sack my walls from within?"

"In a manner of speaking."

She ran her tongue over her teeth, and he wasn't sure he wanted to know what words she was holding back. He wasn't sure it would do either one of them any good if he found he really could read her. How would that change the past? Or the future?

He should have let her leave.

"Troy is my son," Madelyn said.

Paris Apollo blinked, not sure he was following this. Or why he felt a kind of unpleasant shift at the notion of the woman he had never forgotten the way he should, with her kind face and wary eyes, as the mother of some other man's son. "Why should one of Ilonia's most decorated ministers concern herself with an American mother? Or better still, deliver her to me?"

"It's more the father of my son that concerns her, I expect."

"And who might the lucky man be?" Paris Apollo asked, already bored with the topic—

But the look on Madelyn's face was like a slap.

And, of course, there was no reason he could conceive of that Angelique Silvestri would bring a random mother to Paris Apollo's attention even if he hadn't been this far up Mount Crotho for two years.

No reason at all.

Save one.

"You?" he demanded, his voice a low growl. "*You* are the mother of my son?"

CHAPTER THREE

THE LAST THING Madelyn wanted to do was tell this man about Troy.

But stubborn as she might have been—and for good or ill, she knew too well that she was terribly stubborn, or she might have attempted to make peace with her parents in the years since Troy had been born instead of imagining various versions of a life-well-lived revenge—she hoped she wasn't a *complete* idiot. There was no way he wouldn't find out everything there was about her son eventually. She was faintly surprised Angelique Silvestri hadn't sent him a dossier already.

Maybe she did and this is a test, she thought then.

Yet even if it was, she'd reasoned that offering him the information of her own volition instead of waiting for it to be dragged out of her might give her *some* edge in this impossible situation.

She regretted the impulse immediately.

And she did not like the tone Paris Apollo took with her. She did not like it one bit.

"I can't tell," she replied, somehow managing to sound cool when everything inside her was at a fever pitch and rising higher by the second, "if you're upset to discover that you have a child…or only that you have a child with *me*."

Those unfathomable green eyes glittered. "Must I choose between the unacceptable and the impossible?"

He sounded…forbidding.

It made Madelyn entirely too aware, in a sudden rush, of the precariousness of her situation here. She wasn't sure how it had escaped her before—except, perhaps, that she had been more focused on the fact that she had not expected she would ever see him again. That she had long ago come to terms with the fact he was a dream she'd had that was forever lost to her.

Or she thought she'd come to terms with it—right up until the moment she'd seen him again.

She hadn't been prepared for that. She could still feel her reaction, skittering all over her skin like a terrible rash.

Madelyn *wished* it was a rash. That Paris Apollo was no more than a spot of poison oak that she could treat with calamine lotion and time.

Instead, she was all alone here, high on a mountain with a man she barely knew. That she'd imagined she did know him once—that she'd fancied herself deeply in love with him—didn't change the fact that he was a stranger to her now. Or that he was unknowable by any metric, a king on a royal island who was bound by nothing at all save his own whims.

Meaning she was bound by the same.

The nearest help—assuming the inscrutable Angelique Silvestri could truly be called *help*—was a long walk down a narrow path, with a steep fall to a gruesome death waiting for the slightest misstep.

King Paris Apollo of Ilonia could do anything he liked with her and there was no one to stop him. Or even argue with him about it.

Something Madelyn really should have thought about before now, she realized. Because he did nothing for long, tense moments but stand there before her, staring at her as if she had betrayed him.

And while he did, she found herself aware of him in a new and newly disconcerting way. It was almost as if she could *smell* his temper the same as she could smell the damp and cold on the wind. She was far too aware of it, like a taste on her tongue. And the fact it kept rising, until even the green of his eyes— so clear and beguiling in all the memories she had of him—seemed stormy.

She had the urge to defend herself. And oh, how she hated herself for the impulse.

"It's time to get out of this weather, I think." But his voice was low as he said it. Dangerous. "Come with me."

He turned then and strode back across the courtyard without so much as a glance over his shoulder to see if she might follow.

And Madelyn had the same internal battle all over again. She could turn on her heel now that he'd walked off. She could run back out that door and then charge down the side of the mountain. She assumed that Angelique Silvestri still waited there, but whether she did or didn't, there was no way to know how she might react to anything Madelyn might do. She might not allow Madelyn back in the vehicle. She might order her to turn around and head right back up to the Hermitage until she'd accomplished whatever it was the older woman imagined Madelyn *could* accomplish here.

There was no safe space. Not here on this island, plunked down in the middle of an uncaring ocean. Maybe not anywhere. The only safe space Madelyn had known since she'd run out of that house in Cambridge was back in Tahoe, there in the little house tucked away in the woods that she shared with her aunt and her son.

There was no use pretending Madelyn hadn't known when she'd left it behind yesterday that she was moving into dangerous, perilous waters. She had. She'd known it with every last cell in her body.

But what choice had she had? The Kingdom of Ilonia had come knocking on her door. There was no more hiding from the reality of Troy's conception. She hadn't seen the point of pretending otherwise.

Because she'd only been foolish for a short while at the end of her time in England.

Madelyn had been relentlessly practical ever since, just as she'd been before her semester abroad.

She knew there was no point backing down now. And no clear way to go about backing down anyway. Angelique Silvestri had made it perfectly clear that not only had the palace known about Madelyn and Troy all this while, but also that no one at the palace had the slightest compunction about doing whatever was deemed necessary to protect the throne.

The older woman had repeated that several times to make certain Madelyn got her meaning.

Your son is the only heir of the King of Ilonia, the older woman had said in that elegantly ferocious manner of hers. *It has suited us to allow him these formative years here, so far away from the eyes of the world. But surely you must always have known that could change in an instant.*

Madelyn had not known any such thing, she thought as she squared her shoulders, shoved her damp hair back from her face, and followed Paris Apollo out of the courtyard, out of the rain, and deep into the jaws of the stone Hermitage. She hadn't known that anyone but her had the faintest idea who the father of her child was. It hadn't occurred to her that anyone cared.

In retrospect, that seemed stupid. She should have known that something like this was inevitable. She should have been prepared for this day to come.

But it had truly never so much as crossed her mind. *So maybe you're not as practical as you like to think*, she chided herself.

Inside the actual building, she was struck at once by the cheerful, sunny light that made the old stone walls seem to glow. It spilled out from sconces in the walls and down from the odd chandelier, making her realize that she'd automatically assumed he would be leading her into some kind of dour stone prison.

Instead, the place was far more welcoming than it looked from the outside. It was so unexpected that she made no objection as she followed him down a long stone hall, made far cozier than she would have imagined possible with old tapestries on the walls to take the chill away. Eventually, Paris Apollo turned into a sort of rambling living room, which was arranged so that all the seating areas faced the wall of windows that must have once been intended for defensive purposes. They had that look, tall and narrow, as if archers had been expected to lurk here, picking off any uninvited guests as they straggled up the steep mountainside.

Paris Apollo still didn't look back at her. Madelyn couldn't decide if that was evidence of his royal arrogance or if he actually didn't care if she'd followed him in or not. She was tempted to think he'd forgotten she was there at all, but he strode to the bar at one end of the room, hefted up a decanter, and poured a deep amber liqueur into two glasses. She watched, feeling something like fragile as he belted his back.

Only when he was duly fortified did he turn to face her, lifting his chin in a mute order for her to come and do the same.

"No, thank you," Madelyn said, with the sort of automatic courtesy that felt like an unwarranted surrender here. Under these circumstances. She cleared her throat and reminded herself that she didn't owe him that. Or anything. "Drinking with you has never led anywhere good."

He let out a laugh at that, but it was nothing more than a scrape of pure bitterness through this room made of stone.

"How old is the child?" he asked her, and that was even worse.

Madelyn felt a rush of reaction inside her then. It took her a breath or two to understand that it was that stubbornness of hers she knew all too well. And possibly a bit of panic, besides.

She didn't want to tell him how old Troy was. She didn't want him to know a single thing about *her son*. She wanted to run, screaming, off this mountain and keep Troy to herself.

But she reminded herself—with some heat—that everything she did here this evening was about being as practical as she'd had to be these last years. Being realistic, no matter what.

And she needed to tread carefully because there was no way to tell how this was going to go, and it didn't matter how she felt about it. It couldn't matter.

Only Troy mattered.

Ever since she'd found out she was carrying him, he was all that mattered.

"Five," she made herself say, in a voice as near to polite as she could manage, and it was a close thing. "He's five years old."

Paris Apollo picked up the glass that had been meant to be hers and tossed that back, too. Then set it back down, the *click* of crystal against stone as loud as a gunshot. "I expected you to say two years. Or even one. That would make sense, Madelyn. Because I have been unreachable during that time. Before that, however, I believe I had the reputation as the most approachable royal in all of Europe."

Madelyn could see those doors again, shut tight at the top of the stairs in that Cambridge house. She could see the pitying yet unmoving expressions on the faces of his guards. She could see Annabel's noxious pity. "You have only ever been as approachable as you wish to be, Paris Apollo, which is not necessarily approachable at all. Whether you remember me or not, let's not pretend otherwise."

He stayed where he was, there on the other end of the room, but she didn't mistake that for anything but what it was—a show of almost unimaginable restraint and, therefore, power. Because she could see the fury crackle all over him. She could taste it in her mouth again. She thought she could even see his muscles shake with the force of all he held inside.

As if she really had dealt him a terrible cruelty here, when that had never been her intention.

The part of her that felt badly for him was no good to her now, she lectured herself then. None of this was his fault, perhaps. But it wasn't hers, either.

When he claimed he didn't even *know who she was*.

"Setting aside the past two years, that leaves three since he was born." He did the math out loud, an obvious challenge. Or a slap. Madelyn stood straighter. "I believe that makes three years and nine preceding months during which you chose not to tell me about this child. Or were you, by any chance, of late in a coma? Unable to use any or all of the time-honored ways of contacting another? A letter. A phone call. An email or text. A bit of skywriting, even. Failing all else, there is always an indiscreet tabloid article."

Madelyn shook her head, astonished to find that she felt a little shaky. Maybe more than a little. "It... never occurred to me to try."

She would have sworn to anyone who would listen that he could never look as dark as he did then, in the way he stared at her. As if she was a monster. "Explain yourself."

Then again, she would also have sworn that he would always be too lazy, too indolent in all ways, to issue orders like that. So fierce and so like a *king* it made her whole body snap to attention, even as that same stubbornness reared its head again inside her.

But she fought it off. Because an explanation was owed to him, like it or not. Madelyn could accept that was true, however little she might like it.

"I was nothing to you." She was distressed to find that was much harder to say out loud than it should have been, all these years later, and the fact he looked almost…surprised to see it made it worse. But she pushed on. "Our affair lasted only a very few weeks. I have no idea what you thought about it, or if you thought about it at all, but I only knew it had ended when your guards barred me from entering your room in Cambridge. When it was very clear that you were otherwise engaged inside."

Words made it seem so…sanitized. A story anyone could tell and likely would, over drinks. The way people liked to do, sharing *dating stories* as if they were badges of dubious honor and funnier the more they were told. Madelyn had heard these stories a thousand times. Her friends—back when she'd had time to spend time with them—had loved nothing more than telling tales like this to amuse each other.

But it had felt as if she was dying.

Something in her had *died* on that landing as surely as if one of the guards had struck her down. She had never been the same, even in those strange months she'd moved through her old life like a ghost, unaware that there was a new life inside of her.

As if the dawning of that hideous understanding of what she and Paris Apollo really were to each other—no matter how deeply she had loved him— really had killed her where she stood.

"So you mean to tell me that it was pettiness, nothing more." His voice was a black ribbon of sound, and it hurt to hear. "The wounded feelings of a jilted lover. This, you felt, was sufficient reason to hide from me the existence of a son for *five years*."

Madelyn felt small and ashamed—but then, nothing she had ever felt about this man was *petty*. Her hands curled into fists, but she made herself carry on.

"I didn't know I was pregnant until I was in the third trimester," she told him quietly, choosing every word with care. "Maybe I didn't want to know." Or maybe she had been little more than a zombie, shuffling through a life that felt like a coffin without him—but she wasn't about to tell him that. That she'd felt ill and unlike herself, certainly, but then again, she'd been deeply depressed. "And once I knew, once I couldn't pretend it was a long flu dragging on or some other ailment, I had other things to think about."

"What else could there possibly be to think about?" he demanded, sounding outraged anew.

"Little things like becoming a single mother," she shot back at him. "My parents wanted me to give up the child for adoption so I could finish college and go on with my life and pretend I was still the dutiful daughter they wanted me to be. When I refused, they washed their hands of me entirely. That meant I had to figure out where I was going to live. How I was going to survive. Oddly enough, those practical considerations consumed me a whole lot more than trying to hunt down a man who'd never really wanted me."

For a moment she thought she heard him growl, all the way from across the room. She told herself that was her guilt talking.

But he looked as if he could happily chew glass all the same. "Did it escape your notice that I'm one of the wealthiest men alive? Did it never occur to you that a single phone call could have solved all your problems?"

It honestly had not. Not once.

"You don't understand," she told him, struggling to keep her upset out of her voice. Because she had thought a lot about this on the long flight over. About what it had been like then, barely twenty-one, back home in California. How could she explain to him what it had been like to go from a small farming town to college in San Francisco? Much less three tumultuous months in a place that had never seemed real, even as she'd walked the streets of Cambridge with her own two feet. And then to have to go back to a San Francisco that had seemed dull and dim in the aftermath of loving him. All that *before* that fateful doctor's appointment where she'd finally faced the truth her body had been shouting at her for months. "To me, those weeks with you were like a fairy tale. The further away I got from them, the more it seemed as if I'd dreamed the whole thing. I had to worry about diapers, not *princes*. And I didn't know how to bridge that gap."

She blew out a breath when he only stared at her with that same dark affront. "After a while, I stopped worrying about *how* I got pregnant because I was having the baby. And I had to figure out how to keep him alive. How to make money and keep a roof over his head. I was lucky enough that my aunt stepped in and helped out. Over the years, we've made it work. We've made a happy little family."

Again, there was nothing but that stare, as if he could not believe she *dared* say these things. Or that she had dared have a whole life out there without notifying him. Madelyn held out her hands, not sure if she was beseeching him or holding him off. "It's not that I *decided* not to tell you, Paris Apollo. I…didn't think of you at all." He stared at her, and she felt her temper ignite. *Finally*, something in her whispered. "Why would I imagine you'd care? *You don't even remember me!*"

But if she thought that would shame him, she was to be dearly disappointed. He only stared back at her as if his own inability to recognize a woman he had once explored so thoroughly that she had written in her diary that he must have tasted every last inch of her body was *her* fault.

Like everything else.

"How extraordinary," he said, harsh and dark, in a way that was laughably out of place for the man she'd met long ago but seemed somehow suited to the man he was here. Surrounded by stone and dressed entirely in black, grim and imposing in every respect. "You expect that I should believe that you have been scrabbling about in the wilds of America, struggling to put a roof over your head, yet…never thought about the fact that I have more roofs than I know what to do with. Is that a pathology, Madelyn? Or merely an attempt to get yours back?"

"Troy is a healthy, happy little boy," Madelyn retorted tightly. "I notice you didn't ask. You couldn't make it clearer that I made the right decision."

Paris Apollo's turquoise gaze seemed to ignite, then go unreadable.

She thought he might pour himself another drink, but he did not. He studied her for a long moment, and then he turned away again, leveling that gaze on the view outside the narrow windows.

What little view there was on a late afternoon tipping over into evening like this one, with a storm settling in.

And somehow his silence made her feel more ashamed than if he'd continued to question her.

She forced her hands open but then didn't know what to do with them, so she clasped them together before her. And inside her head, she found herself running through excuses…when, if she was blameless, she shouldn't need any.

Was he right? Had it truly never occurred to her to tell him simply because their stations were so far apart, as she'd believed? Or had she been an angry, vengeful woman scorned all along?

How could she not know for certain?

Madelyn hated that after all this time, after living her life far away from him and coming to enjoy it on its own merits, it took only this little stretch of time with him before she couldn't tell.

"You said we met at Cambridge." He kept his attention trained out the windows. "I met a great many women at Cambridge."

That spiraling sensation of shame disappeared, swallowed up in a bright, hot surge of temper. And the memory of Annabel's smirking English-rose face. "Believe me, I am aware."

"Am I to assume you were a student there?"

"I was there for a semester," she said, ignoring that insinuation she was sure she could hear in his voice. That she might not have been a student at lofty Cambridge like him, given her *cheap shoes* and general *commonness*. That she was so below him and his ilk that she must have had some other reason for being there—perhaps in some lowly service job like the one she had now. Thoughts she'd had herself while she was there, even before she'd met him, but it was different to imagine *him* thinking them, too. It made her stomach hurt. "It was an exchange program."

"You said it was an affair, did you not? Therefore not a single night. Is that so?"

"It was several weeks," she told him stiffly. "And, apparently, wholly unmemorable. Thank you for continuing to dwell on something so unpleasant and embarrassing."

"What I am trying to discern," Paris Apollo bit out, quietly but furiously, "is whether or not you knew who I was. By which I mean, Crown Prince Paris Apollo, the heir apparent to the Ilonian throne."

"Everyone knows who you are. Everyone *knew* who you were."

"So, truly, you have no excuse for failing to tell me." His back was so rigid, as if he'd grown even taller than his six feet and at least three inches while they talked. "Any father should be told he has child, but surely it should have dawned upon you that a man with an inevitable throne in his future has more than a mere passing interest in any potential heirs."

"No," Madelyn said, with great precision that she hoped masked the great mess within her. "While out of my mind from the lack of sleep, the fact that my parents disowned me, and no idea how I was going to feed my baby, I did not stop and think about the royal line of succession in the country that—and I don't mean this is an insult—is very rarely mentioned where I come from. Your exploits are one thing. Everyone likes a scandalous rich man, forever behaving atrociously. But the details of who gets to take a throne and when? Not so much."

Paris Apollo only nodded at that, but not as if he was agreeing. More as if he was simply…taking it on board. Building a picture. No doubt to condemn her even more, she could only imagine.

"Where is the child now?"

She scowled at his back. "At home. Where he belongs. With my aunt, who's been helping me care for him since he was tiny. I think I told you that already."

"And where is home? Exactly?"

Madelyn didn't want to tell him. But even as she thought that, she knew it was foolish. It was one more thing she wasn't likely to be able to keep to herself. It was already too late. All he would need to do was get in touch with his minister and she would tell him anything he wanted to know.

Again, there was probably a dossier en route as they spoke.

So Madelyn made herself smile, suddenly pleased with her choice of profession. She'd been waiting tables for years now and had learned how to smile serenely no matter the provocation. Who could have imagined that serving the tables of self-important and often overtly wealthy skiers would turn out to be such a useful skill?

"I live in a tiny town near Lake Tahoe," she told him, keeping her tone even. Calm. "If you don't know it, Lake Tahoe is a very large and beautiful lake on the border between California and Nevada in the Sierra Nevadas, notable for its ski resorts, its rustic charm, and its stunning scenery. There are quite a lot of tourists and resorts on the lake, in all seasons. I actually live a bit further out, in the hills."

Where life was much more affordable. Most of her neighbors worked on the lake the way she did but, like her, preferred a little space between themselves and the relentless influx of visitors requiring service.

Paris Apollo did not question her further on the demographics of Lake Tahoe. He turned back to face her and seemed to be content to do nothing but study her while the silence grew. A muscle clenched and unclenched in his jaw, as if somewhere beneath the surface, that temper she could still scent in the air between them was getting the best of him.

Madelyn couldn't imagine the Paris Apollo she'd known having any kind of temper at all, but if he had, she would've expected him to simply...blow up. Then blow over. She would have imagined he would share it with anyone and everyone who drew near. She would have said he was incapable of all this *simmering control.*

But then, it wasn't as if she needed further confirmation that she hardly knew him at all.

For some reason, that made her want to attack him, so she did it the only way she could think of. "Why are you really hiding away up here? I understand grieving. But two years seems like a very long time away from the spotlight for a man who grew up hogging it."

She knew, instantly, that she'd said the wrong thing.

Or the right thing, maybe. Because Paris Apollo seemed to change before her eyes once again. And the more she looked at this new version of him— hard and grim, like he truly was fashioned from rock—the harder it was to remember the man she'd known so long ago. Back when she'd been a foolish girl who still believed in fairy tales and Prince Charmings. Before she'd known how badly a broken, trampled heart could hurt inside her ribs. Before she'd known anything.

She wouldn't trade a single moment of Troy's life or the joy he'd brought her—but still, she found it hard to reconcile herself with the naive creature she'd been six years ago.

And Paris Apollo was looking at her now as if she was something else entirely.

Something like an enemy.

There was no reason at all that it should make her…shivery.

She tamped down on that reaction.

Hard.

"During these years you've hidden away, have you had contact with any other Ilonians?" he asked, in a steel-tipped voice.

"I have never met an Ilonian in my entire life except you. Until the day that Angelique Silvestri appeared at my front door, which was yesterday. I think. There have been a great many time zones since."

His green gaze seemed far darker than it looked. "You are certain of this?"

"I am not *certain*, no. I wait tables in luxury hotels, Paris Apollo. In case you don't know what that is, or what that means, I'm a waitress." She waited for him to curl his lip, but he didn't. He only watched her, much too closely. Much too *intently*, and she wasn't sure that was better. Though it made that shivery thing inside her intensify. "But there are always rich men with this or that accent, throwing their money around. I don't actually take the time to interrogate them about where they're from. I'm a little more focused on doing my job, because I want good tips. That's the entire point of waiting tables."

"What of your personal life?" His gaze got even sharper somehow. Even darker. "Do you often entertain men?"

Madelyn actually laughed at that. "I entertain one man. He's very demanding. He doesn't leave a lot of room for others." When Paris Apollo only glowered at her, she scowled back at him. "My son. I mean *my son*. Obviously."

"If Angelique could find you, anyone could." But it sounded like he was talking to himself. "I must assume that they did."

"She told me the palace has always known each and every woman you have ever been involved with. Meaning *you* may not remember me, but I believe I'm on a very long list kept by someone who does." She shrugged with a carelessness she certainly did not feel. Though she thought she ought to. "For all you know, you might have hundreds of sons kicking around out there."

And that would be a good thing, surely. Because then he wouldn't need to concern himself with hers. But the way her stomach turned over inside her, it almost seemed as if a pretty sizeable portion of her didn't think that was a *good thing* at all.

She shoved it aside, though it took a great deal of

effort. "But you still haven't answered the question I asked you. Two years up here, all alone, seems the most unlike-you thing I could possibly imagine. You must have a reason."

"Grieving the loss of both my parents at once, and following my culture's custom while I do so, does not strike you as a sufficient reason?"

But Madelyn didn't back down at that as she was clearly meant to. "I lost my parents, too, you know. The fact they're still alive, as far as I know, isn't as much of a comfort as it should be. I'm not suggesting it's the same, but I'm also not sure that hiding away on a mountaintop is any kind of healthy."

Then she found herself holding her breath. Because he prowled toward her and there was no part of him that reminded her of that languid, pleasure-seeking creature she'd known in Cambridge. This man was some kind of rangy, beguiling predator. Even the way he moved was different. Not *languid* at all. As if everything about him was as hard as rock, inside and out.

Once again, all she could think was that he'd made himself into some kind of weapon. And that weapon was aimed directly at her.

She should probably have more of a reaction than that exultant, *shivering* thing inside her.

He stopped when he was much too close. Madelyn felt her heart in her throat, pounding so hard she was surprised she didn't choke, as he reached over—

She wanted to squeak out a protest. She wanted to

turn and run. Or maybe she wanted to throw herself into his arms instead. But she had more than just herself to think about now, so she stood fast, planted her feet in the ground, and didn't move an inch.

Somehow, she faced him. Somehow, she didn't run.

Or worse, surrender to that longing that had already been her undoing once before.

And she had never been more aware of anything in her life, so intense and so darkly hot, as the way he reached over, took a bit of her damp hair between his fingers, and tucked it behind her ears.

It should have been a sweet, kind thing to do. Tender, even. Affectionate.

But she could see the expression on his face.

She could feel the way it knocked through her, making her knees feel weak. Making a strange heat bloom behind her eyes and a matching one deep between her legs.

"My parents were murdered," he told her, his voice as dark as the gathering night outside. And she could feel it inside her, too, as if he was a rainstorm, pounding its way through her. Drenching her. Growing stronger and wilder with every moment. "And everyone responsible will pay. I have not spent these years catering to my feelings, Madelyn. I have been preparing myself for the battle ahead. And I tell you this now. If I discover that you have anything to do with what befell them—"

"Are you... Are you accusing me of *murdering*

your parents?" It came out in a whisper because that was all she could manage. "*Me?* A waitress from halfway around the world?"

"You call yourself a waitress, but what Angelique has proved is that you are a pawn," Paris Apollo told her, almost softly. "But the trouble with pawns is that they can be played by anyone. It will not go well for you if it turns out you have been embroiled in the plots I intend to expose."

"I have nothing to do with these games you're playing," she managed to say. She felt a kind of wildfire power move inside her that she knew came entirely from being a mother. Troy's mother. Because even here, high up the side of a mountain, in a place she hoped her son would never visit, she would protect him. She didn't care about herself, but she would protect him if it took her final breath. No matter what reaction she might be having to the man who'd fathered him. "I want nothing to do with them. You didn't know you had a son before today and really, there's no reason for you to involve yourself with him at all. He's fine. He has a good life. He's happy and he's loved. The last thing in the world he needs is to be caught up in…whatever this is."

She waved her hand between them, only realizing after she'd done it that it was a rough approximation of the careless way she remembered him waving his hand back in England. To indicate his boredom. To bring people closer to him or send them away.

To remind everyone at all times how languid and yet above them all he was.

What she didn't expect was for Paris Apollo to catch her hand in his.

For a moment, there was nothing between them but the touch of his flesh to hers. The heat of his hand, flooding her with too many memories to bear.

That mad fire that had burned her alive—and worse, she'd liked it.

"I suggest you make yourself comfortable," he told her in that low, too-dangerous voice of stone and darkness. "It is pitch-black outside and there are no lights to mark the trail. It is too treacherous to attempt tonight."

"I'm not staying here. That was never… I didn't agree to that."

He ignored that outburst. "If you follow this hall to the far end, you will find the kitchen. Feel free to help yourself to anything that appeals to you. If you wish to rest—and I suggest you do—there are many chambers to choose from." The words he used sounded almost welcoming, but his tone reminded her of bullets. One after the next, and none of them anything but deadly. "Pick any you like."

Paris Apollo stepped away from her then, but it seemed as if it took him a little too long to drop her hand. Or maybe it only seemed that way to her because she could *feel* too much. Or because she wanted him to feel something. Anything.

And then, when he did finally drop her hand, she could still feel it, and that was incalculably worse.

"You have had five years to make all the decisions you liked," he said quietly. Too quietly, when his eyes blazed the way they did. When she still felt like a tattered bit of target practice, and worse, like the lover he'd discarded years ago—but as if it had just happened anew. "It seems you made all the wrong ones. But that time has ended. And now, Madelyn, I am afraid that both you and I must suffer the consequences of the decisions I have already made."

Then, to her astonishment, he actually turned and left her there.

And she didn't see him again until morning.

When a helicopter landed on the top of the Hermitage and the King of Ilonia informed her with a particular glittering look in his pale green eyes that they were headed back to the palace at last…

But it was if she'd brought something terrible upon herself, not as if she'd won.

CHAPTER FOUR

THE HELICOPTER FLEW them down from the Hermitage, across the sea, and in low over the old harbor and ancient city that clung to the cliffs below the palace.

Where it seemed the entire kingdom of Ilonia had taken to the streets to greet them.

Madelyn thought she was having a kind of panic attack, but it was impossible to tell if all that wild roaring was coming from inside her or the throngs of cheering Ilonians down below. Because even from high up in the air, the celebrations in the streets were loud enough to be heard over the rotors and reverberate inside her body.

Making her feel dangerously, hectically *alive*.

It made her ask herself what on earth she was doing here.

With him.

It had been a long night. She'd spent the first part of it convinced that Paris Apollo was testing her in some way and was in all likelihood watching her as she tried to decide what to do. She'd wheeled around and headed outside once he left her, not trusting him at all. But when she'd rushed across the stone court and through the door to the outside of the Hermitage's walls, she saw he'd told her no more than the truth.

The night had come in fast. The hail that had turned to rain and then back again didn't help. She might have braved the trail anyway, but he hadn't been lying about the light and weather situation, either. Madelyn could not see a thing outside the Hermitage walls. She could barely see her hand in front of her own face. She told herself she could hug the side of the mountain as she went down, and she could creep along as slowly as she liked—

But the same problems remained. First, she had more than her feelings to consider, which should have been the only thing that mattered to her. Second, even if she didn't topple off the side as she slipped downhill, there was no telling if anyone waited for her in that parking area halfway up the mountain. If no one was there, that meant she would be stranded, alone and outside on this island for the night. For the night or even longer, depending on whether or not anyone decided to look for her.

Depending on when or *if* Paris Apollo noticed she was gone, then did or did not raise an alarm.

And as much as she might have liked to make a point by doing exactly that, she couldn't.

Because she had to think about Troy, not just her damned wounded pride.

So Madelyn had turned around, located her spine, and marched stiffly back inside the Hermitage. Then she'd made her first order of business finding a room with a decent lock.

Though she wasn't quite certain if she wanted to lock Paris Apollo out...or herself in.

It had been a bit lowering to discover that there were a great many rooms with dead bolts aplenty. She chose one, locked herself in, and then sat there for some time. Like all the other rooms she'd peeked into, the chamber she'd picked was comfortably and simply furnished. Despite the actual *King* in residence, this was not a place of overwhelming opulence. That surprised her. The furniture was sturdy, the rugs cozy, and in some rooms, there were fireplaces that leapt to life at the touch of a button.

If she'd had any other reason for being there, she probably would have loved it.

Once she'd gotten herself warm and dry in front of the fire, she'd followed her hunger pangs down to the kitchen, where she found food and drink. As promised. It was all simple and easy and good. Fresh-baked bread. Hard cheese and savory sausages. She'd fixed herself a plate, then headed back to her room, furtively, expecting Paris Apollo to appear at any moment—

But he hadn't.

Not even when she had thought she heard him—not that she could imagine the famously lethargic Paris Apollo *running* through the stone halls or moving heavy things about, as it sounded like he was doing at one point.

Madelyn had told herself it was the wind.

And she'd talked herself out of wandering around the halls later to see if she could find him. She'd decided that would suggest a level of interest in him and his activities that she didn't wish to convey.

No matter that she might feel exactly that level of interest and more.

Also, the way he'd looked at her as if *she* was the monster who had betrayed *him*—and she could see why he might feel that way, as unfair as it felt to her after she'd been the one to struggle through Troy's birth and infancy on her own while he appeared in tabloids, wearing supermodels like so many cloaks, not that she'd looked—made her think that perhaps she'd be better off making sure she didn't provoke him.

She slept fitfully, dark and odd and fire-licked dreams in her head, and woke to the sound of the helicopter in the distance.

The flight across the sweep of the Ilonian islands was beautiful. An aching kind of beauty, the sort that didn't make her want to drink cocktails and dance on white-sand beaches but rather…wander about in the wild, lonely, desolate far reaches of these moody islands.

Until you find yourself, she thought.

And then had to sit with how strange that thought was. As she wasn't lost. She didn't have the time or the privilege to *lose herself*, and if she did, it wouldn't be *here*.

With the man who brooded in the seat beside her.

"What are we doing here?" she asked him as they climbed out of the helicopter on the landing pad adjacent to the palace.

"I suspect you can work that out," was his reply, in the same harsh voice he'd used since yesterday.

But then, as he turned and walked toward the scrum of palace aids and ministers—if the presence of Angelique Silvestri was any guide—Madelyn watched him...change.

It was only then that she realized he wasn't dressed the way he had been the night before. Gone were the black clothes, utilitarian and simple, but it was more than that. It wasn't only the less-fitted clothing he wore now that somehow broadcast its own astronomical expense. The way he'd dressed in Cambridge, now that she thought about it. Like then, she couldn't have said *why* the pair of trousers and shirt he wore were any different from any other, only that they were. They very clearly had been made for him specifically. Likely by hand. And every step he took was a quiet whisper of the kind of offhanded male elegance that was only possible with unlimited funds.

Madelyn could have spent some time fuming over that, but she tucked it away because it wasn't *just* the clothes. She studied him, trailing behind him, as he strode toward his people. It was the way he moved. It was the way he smiled.

It was the fact that he smiled at all.

But it wasn't until she saw him wave that languid hand of his that she understood what he was doing. He was reverting back to type. Becoming that easy playboy of a prince she'd met long ago.

The Prince his people expected, perhaps.

She watched, strange suspicions gripping her, as he was welcomed home in a series of deep curtsies and informal bows. A rippling wave of them as he walked from the helicopter across the grand forecourt, and not the way he'd moved around the Hermitage last night.

This version of Paris Apollo...sauntered. Madelyn followed at a distance, aware that it was likely no coincidence that she was quickly flanked by a selection of royal guards as she moved, but she didn't mind that. Maybe she should have, but she was too busy watching Paris Apollo as he put on his show.

By the time they made it inside, she understood that he was striking a note somewhere between that grim, gruff man from the Hermitage and the lazy, pleasure-seeking wastrel he'd been when she'd so foolishly fallen for him in Cambridge. The one she'd seen in all those tabloids afterward.

But she didn't have the chance to ask him which one was real, because once inside, he was swept away in the crowd of staff and ministers and she was marched off to a set of rooms that, a cheerful woman of indeterminate rank and position told her, were to be hers.

"For the duration," the woman said.

"I don't need *rooms*," Madelyn replied, fighting to sound nothing more than polite. "I need a plane. I brought you back your king and now I need to go home."

The woman only laughed, then left her standing in the large foyer of the expansive apartment. And when Madelyn checked her door, she found there were two guards standing on the other side.

"Am I a prisoner?" she asked them.

Maybe less politely than she planned.

"His Majesty requests that you stay in these rooms," replied one of the guards.

"So that, madam, is what you'll do," said the other. Sternly.

Madelyn went back inside, indulged herself and her panic for moment, then tried to *think*.

Unlike the Hermitage, the palace was sumptuous in every detail. From the moldings on the ceiling with set-in illustrations to the sumptuous brocaded window dressings, she could not have felt more out of place if she'd found herself on the moon.

She made her way over to the windows—a little shakily—and looked out over the island. It looked green and lush today and far more welcoming than the great mountain she'd climbed yesterday. The sea danced in every direction so that there was no part of the island that didn't seem to also be a part of all those waves and the beaches they threw themselves against, over and over again.

And she could hear the celebrations from the city streets even before she found her way to a pair of French doors and stepped out onto her balcony.

She felt the sun on her face. She heard the songs in the air. And she couldn't have said why it was that the people's joyful response to the return of their king made her feel so…emotional. When she shouldn't have cared. What was it to her what these people felt about Paris Apollo coming down off his mountaintop? It didn't change the fact that she was imprisoned here, did it?

Or the fact that she had no idea what he intended to do with her.

Or, worse, with Troy.

The panic beat at her again. She had nothing of her own with her, not even her bag. Or the cell phone inside it. Madelyn wheeled around and pushed her way back inside, moving almost frantically until she found an ornate, old-style rotary phone on one of the side tables in the living room. She picked it up, half expecting to find an operator there who would act like one of the guards and refuse to put her call through—

But she heard a dial tone. And she still remembered how to make international calls from her time in England, so that was what she did, keying in her aunt's number and waiting impatiently as the rotary slowly cycled out each number. And then rang.

And rang. And rang.

She tried three more times as the hours ticked by, but there was no answer.

And no matter how many times she told herself that all was well—and she was getting the time change wrong, that was all—she was…not okay.

When the doors to her rooms were tossed open, she fully expected to see Angelique Silvestri standing there. And perhaps a brass band, now that she thought about it, because she had gone and done the exact thing that she'd been asked to do. Surely all that was left now was to be congratulated, then escorted to a plane so she could fly back home and hug her kid.

Instead, a group of cheerful, chattering women came in, pushing a rolling rack of clothes with them.

"It's time to dress you," cried one of the women. "On this happiest and most auspicious of days!"

Madelyn looked more closely at the rack as they rolled it over toward her and saw that it was stuffed full of dresses. Beautiful dresses, it had to be said, but something inside her turned over and went cold.

"I don't need to get dressed. I am dressed." She sounded odd and strained. Even she could hear it. "For traveling, which is handy because I need to go home."

Another one of the women smiled even more broadly than the first. "King Paris Apollo has finally returned to his people. It is a day for celebrating, not for traveling. And as you are in the palace, an honored guest of His Majesty, it would be better if you were dressed like everyone else. Don't you think?"

Madelyn couldn't really argue the logic in that, so she didn't put up a fight. She told herself it wasn't so much that she was surrendering so much as conserving her energy for bigger fights to come.

She didn't ask herself how she knew they were coming. Though the blaze of Paris Apollo's green eyes seemed to light her up inside all the same. Even if only in her memories from last night.

Though she kept that shivering thing locked down tight, deep inside.

And so she let the women lead her deeper into the apartment that she hadn't bothered to explore, until they reached an expansive walk-in closet that opened up into the kind of dressing room she'd only ever seen on reality shows. Certainly not in real life. They sat her down on a little bench before a mirror—it was called a vanity, wasn't it?—and fussed all around her, talking over her head and giving her entirely too much time to think.

It wasn't the dresses that put her off. It was that the last time she'd fussed over pretty things, and watched herself so closely in mirrors, was back when this game of dominoes had begun, one tipping the other over, on and on, until there was Troy.

And now her presence here, in a *palace*, of all things.

Madelyn decided that the only thing to do was to think of it in terms of the story she would tell Troy of her adventures here. She could tell him that she'd been a bit of a Cinderella for a few days. He would love it.

The three women settled on a palette they all liked, after holding up a variety of fabrics and shades and studying Madelyn's reflection with great intensity. They did her hair. They applied more cosmetics than Madelyn had ever owned. They had her step into a dress, and then they sewed it a bit here and there for the perfect fit.

Madelyn told herself she didn't care, that it was all part of the story she would tell her son later, but she did sneak sideways looks at every mirror they passed once they led her from the room.

Because maybe she wasn't immune to Cinderella stories, little as she'd like to admit that.

And as they led her out of the guest wing and into the more public parts of the palace, she conceded—privately—that she really would have felt out of place if she were dressed in the clothes she'd worn on the plane. Everyone else seemed effortlessly chic and elegant, even the people who were very clearly staff.

"Where are you taking me?" she thought to ask when she finally found her voice. When the dazzling splendor of the great palace all around released its grip on her somewhat.

But only somewhat.

"This is the new wing," one of the women told her. "It was thought you would be more comfortable there, being American and all. Americans like new things, don't they?"

"I…" She'd been about to argue, but Madelyn stopped herself. The truth was, she'd stood in buildings in Cambridge that were hundreds of years older than even the oldest buildings in the States. She had no idea how old this palace was, but clearly, Ilonia had been around for centuries. "I suppose we do like new things."

The women all looked pleased at that. Madelyn was pleased in turn, until one of them breathed, "His Majesty is so thoughtful and wise."

But there was no time to argue the point. They walked faster then, crossing through one marble courtyard and leading her down halls festooned with dazzling mirrors and paintings the size of walls, then leading her into a vast room that felt like it was outside though it wasn't. It took her breath. Because on one end, there was nothing but the sea and sky, there just beyond the walls of glass. And on the other end, there was a gleaming throne set high on a raised dais, arranged beneath a trellis made of gold and marble and the kind of backdrop that made her think of organs in cathedrals.

King Paris Apollo stood there, dressed in ceremonial robes.

And for a moment, Madelyn felt light-headed. As if every bit of blood inside her body deserted her. As if she'd fallen off that narrow trail after all and was even now hurtling down the steep side of that cold mountain.

Because it was one thing to understand who Paris Apollo was. To know, intellectually, that he had been a prince in Cambridge. That he had become a king two years ago, however tragically.

But in all the interactions she'd had with him, in and out of that bed of his in Cambridge, what he'd been to her was unfathomably rich. That was all. He had also been equally unfathomably beautiful and perfect, but she hadn't spent time thinking about *thrones* and *kingdoms*.

Words like *prince* or *king* had been just that. Words.

Now there was no pretending. He looked like every painting of a monarch she'd ever seen. Every history book, every movie. There was a crown on his head. He wore fussy robes of red and white that somehow seemed to make him look more attractive when he should have looked as if he was playing dress-up. In one hand, he even held a scepter.

Madelyn's throat went dry. She felt her heart beat hard, deep inside her, as if it was trying to knock her sideways. It took her much too long to even notice that this particular vast hall of a room was crowded. There were seats set up in the center, with rows of cameras lined up behind them, and so many *people*. And yet she was glad of the bustle of it all as her attendants led her to a front-row seat at the foot of the wide stairs that led to the throne.

She was grateful to be seated that far away from the cameras and all the curious eyes on her, because she had to do something with her face. All she felt was overly red and somehow vulnerable. Exposed. As if finally seeing Paris Apollo for who he really was—who he had always been—meant she was revealed as well.

Don't be silly, she told herself sharply, though that didn't much help. *There is nothing to reveal.*

She wasn't the one with a questionable memory. She had no secrets here.

Up on his dais, Paris Apollo was surrounded by a great many men and women dressed in fine dresses and many black suits, all of them holding folders or clipboards and frowning self-importantly. She found herself holding her breath as she studied him, as if looking for clues. Maybe she was. Maybe she thought that if she could find that long-ago lover in the King who stood above her now, all of this would make sense. Or even that man from last night, harsh and accusatory, yet somehow more accessible than the *King* he was now.

Because even dressed in robes and a *crown*, this Paris Apollo was smiling. He seemed almost approachable, when he should have seemed anything but. It was the same thing she'd noticed earlier. As if he was somehow bridging the gap between the versions of him she'd already met.

But thinking about that made her feel dizzy again, so she twisted in her seat and looked out once more to where the back wall seemed to dissolve into all that glass, creating a kind of optical illusion. As if the sky and the sea were in the palace with them, crowning the King in all that blue.

Madelyn knew that the palace sat high on a hill. She knew that if she went to the wall of windows and looked out, she would gaze down into the city that stretched out all the way down that hill, over the cliffs, and down into the harbor.

But from up here, it looked as if the Ilonian palace was the only thing in all the world.

Certainly the only thing mattered.

As if the King who ruled here was some kind of god of the sea.

Looking at Paris Apollo again, she felt much the same. Dizzy. Awed.

All those things she'd felt that fateful night in the pub but had since pretended had only been her inexperience.

No, she thought now. *It's just him. It's always been him.*

He had seemed like a god to her then. There was a part of her that hadn't been at all surprised when he'd moved on the way he did—because who had she been kidding? He was *him*. She was her. The gulf between them had always been too wide and too deep to cross.

Madelyn was just lucky that, for a short little while, she'd gotten to touch him.

Maybe she needed to find a way to be grateful for that.

A loud sort of gong sounded, and the crowd went still and quiet. Up on the stage, all the attendants faded away before the gong did, leaving Paris Apollo standing by himself.

With only his throne. And his crown.

Madelyn expected him to take his seat, but he did not. She looked around for the usual ubiquitous teleprompters anyone would expect in a situation like this, but saw nothing. It made her ribs hurt to realize it was just Paris Apollo up there, all by himself.

"My fellow Ilonians," he began, "my beloved Islanders, it is my joy and privilege to show you not only that I am alive and well, but that I have spent these years of grief and mourning making myself over into the King you deserve."

Sitting this close to his stage, it was too easy to forget about that harder, grimmer man she'd encountered at the Hermitage. It was tempting to believe the conviction in his voice and in his gaze.

Yet Madelyn held her breath as he spoke, and she wasn't sure why. He was saying reasonable things. He was talking about hopes and dreams. Of his kingdom, of his promises. Of his lost parents.

And the longer he spoke, the more the spell of this hall and his *scepter* eased its grip on her. Belatedly, it occurred to her that there was no reason at all that she should be sitting in the *front row* for his first speech to his people. She wasn't Ilonian. She wasn't anything. And given the tenor of the conversation that she and Paris Apollo had had the night before, she couldn't imagine he *wanted* her here. She really ought to have been surprised that he hadn't left her locked up for the duration. Maybe even in the dungeons.

She assumed all palaces had dungeons.

"I am well aware that there are many who, no matter their affection for my family or even for myself, question whether I am ready to make these commitments to you," Paris Apollo intoned. And he smiled. "My parents indulged me. I indulged myself. But those days are gone. With my father and mother. And there is no greater way to honor them, in my mind, than to become the son I know they anticipated that I would become in time."

Then he moved to the edge of the dais, his gaze upon Madelyn, and started down the wide stairs until he stood before her. His hand outstretched while she…froze in horror.

She had no intention of taking it.

But the women on either side of her made excited noises, and before she knew it—without committing to any movement at all—she found herself on her feet.

Because, of course, she'd been placed right here at the bottom of the stairs on purpose. Right here where everyone could see her. Right here while the cameras tracked Paris Apollo's every move.

Paris Apollo took her hand in his and led her up

the stairs, somehow making what should have been an awkward and embarrassing moment feel as graceful as a dance. When they stood once more before his throne, before the crowd, his green eyes found hers and held.

And like a terrible curse, Madelyn could feel him everywhere.

Everywhere.

That shiver took her over, and she could feel him in ways that reminded her of things best forgotten. Best left in the past and never thought of during the light of day. Or in public. Things better locked away, like those dreams she sometimes had—

Stop, she ordered herself desperately.

This was probably her trial and execution, and here she was getting *overheated.* It was embarrassment on top of embarrassment.

Worse, she could tell he knew.

But he was turning to the crowd and speaking again.

"It is my great honor to present to you the future Queen of Ilonia," Paris Apollo said in a voice that sounded as if it could have carried all the way to the sea without any microphone. As if perhaps it carried across the sea, too.

And for a moment, Madelyn glanced around, expecting some other woman to step forward and thinking that this was really the ultimate slap, wasn't it? It was as if she could see that awful Annabel in her head again, smirk at the ready...

But no other woman rose or came toward the dais.

Once again, it took entirely too long for the penny to drop. Her first reaction was a rush of something far too much like joy for a woman who knew exactly what Paris Apollo's promises were worth. Then she had the stray, strange thought that maybe if she became a queen, her parents might finally be proud of her again. But even as she thought that, her temper kicked in.

But as it did, she saw a slight disturbance back near the glass walls. Just the faintest movement, back behind the cameras.

Madelyn's blood turned to ice in her veins as she saw her aunt Corrine, smiling in her usual cheerful way. And worse, the little boy with her, looking a little bit sleepy and distinctly sulky, likely because he didn't want to admit how tired he clearly was—

"You can't do this," she hissed at Paris Apollo over the applause and cheers that greeted his announcement. She hadn't even noted the crowd's reaction, so busy looking for appropriate queens and finding Troy instead.

"I think you'll find I can," Paris Apollo returned silkily, his hand moving to cover the mic she hadn't even seen clipped to one of his robes. "I suggest you smile, little Queen. You are so good at it."

And what could Madelyn do? He had trapped her. Corrine was bent down, whispering in Troy's ear. Troy had clearly seen her himself, because he was smiling wide and looked as if he might break at any moment and run for her.

Madelyn would never forgive Paris Apollo for this. To risk her son in this way. To throw him like so much meat before these vultures, exposing him to the world—

"In the days to come," the King was saying then, as if blissfully unaware of what he was doing to her, "I hope that you will not only come to know my Madelyn as I do, but will come to love her as your own." He took her hand, the one he'd been holding all this time, and lifted it to his lips. And when he saw the murder that she knew had to be all over her face, he only smiled. "We will be wed within the month."

And it was not until the gong rang again that Madelyn realized he had tricked her.

That Troy was not here so that Paris Apollo could expose him, but to ensure she kept her silence while he made his announcements.

Worse, it had worked. Because now, like it or not, the entire world thought she was engaged to marry the King of Ilonia.

Leaving Madelyn well and truly trapped with the man—the *King*—who she had failed to tell was the father of her son.

And whatever he might decide to do about it.

CHAPTER FIVE

PARIS APOLLO THOUGHT he was keeping himself together masterfully, if he said so himself. And he was King now. What he said was as good as law.

Yet he had underestimated how hard it would be to come back to the palace.

Where his parents were not and never would be again.

And he had been unprepared for how difficult it would be to see his own flesh and blood, his *son*, and not react. Not even approach him, there in that crowd, because it would draw too much attention to the child and it wasn't time yet. Not yet.

Not until he'd come to a better place with...all of it.

He had even underestimated his own reaction to claiming Madelyn as his future queen, something that sat uneasily on him even now. It had not felt like the chess move he'd thought it would. It had not felt *tactical*. It had been significantly more *tactile*, in fact.

Paris Apollo had taken her hand, there at the foot of the stairs that led up to the dais, and it was as if the years had melted away. As if he was still that fool who had imagined futures with Madelyn. The same idiot who had thought he was more to her than just another European landmark, easily checked off a list and forgotten before the plane taxied down the runway at Heathrow.

As if he was still the man who had taken her innocence and had intended to claim her as his, for good.

It had all washed through him as if it was new, as wild and deep and darkly *right*—

But he held it all tightly bound within him. It was one more thing he'd learned how to do these last cold years.

He told himself it didn't matter if anyone else noticed. Even this woman, who he kept reacting to as if he wanted her to know that he remembered her all too well. No matter how he tried to pretend otherwise, there was that deeply buried thread of need and hunger in him, a glimmer of gold that he did his best to tamp down and forget.

Paris Apollo assured himself there was no gold in him. There was no room for such fripperies. There was only and ever vengeance.

This was what he told himself later that same night.

"How *dare* you *kidnap* my child and parade him into the middle of this circus of yours?" Madelyn was demanding, flushed with fury. "Then use him as a weapon against me? I don't know what happened to make you so delusional, Paris Apollo—though my money's on isolating yourself in a stone cage for two years—but I'm certainly not *marrying* you."

Paris Apollo took all that as yet another sign that everything was going swimmingly. And better yet, precisely as planned. Which was good because the plan had been…more difficult to execute than expected.

He had finished his introductory speech to his people. He'd taken all the necessary pictures and spoken to all the reporters. He'd introduced Madelyn, announced her as his future queen, and seen the child—*his child*—with his own eyes.

Something in him had shifted uncomfortably at the sight of the boy, looking too much like the pictures Paris Apollo had seen of himself at that age for comfort. He'd had the strangest urge to just…go to him, as if he was not in the midst of the most critical performance of his life. As if he would know what to do with a child.

As if, deep down, he recognized his own blood. At a glance.

Or maybe it was that longing in him for family that had been like an open wound in him for two endless years—

But he had not succumbed to the urge. Because the child was there to put pressure on Madelyn, not to be presented to the world as Paris Apollo's heir.

That needed to happen at precisely the right time.

He had been up the whole of the previous night, working through every possible scenario and all potential outcomes.

The boy's presence was all part of his plan and was all about exerting his will on this woman. It had nothing to do with the *what ifs* that plagued him.

He couldn't allow fantasies of the family he didn't deserve, not after treating his original one so shabbily, to get in the way of the reckoning he planned to deliver to his loathsome cousin. He would not permit himself to succumb to the lure of the boy, no matter how much he wished he could.

Precisely *because* he wished he could.

The aide in charge of ushering the child into the great hall at the right moment took the boy and Madelyn's aunt out again at the King's nod. When Paris Apollo's speech was done, he had allowed Madelyn's attendants to take her to their son—*his son*—because he'd assumed that would be the only thing she'd want to do.

What he had not anticipated was that it might be what he wanted to do, too.

Paris Apollo had been so sure that he had thought through every possible avenue, but he had not imagined that he would feel this deep, abiding *need* within him to put his hands on the *person* he had made with Madelyn.

It made him feel as close to drunk as he'd been in years.

Now the sun was setting over the palace. His

home, though it felt new around him after having been gone so long. And having made the excesses of Europe his home for so long before that.

He wanted it to hurry up and get dark. Really dark, so he could begin the second, more hands-on phase of his plan. The part he'd trained for all this time. All those things he'd taught himself to do, high up on that unwelcoming mountain, with no one around to pay attention to the kinds of physical feats the grieving King was learning to execute at will.

He had made himself a creature of the night. A weapon who could do the things that protocol and tradition and the sluggish and inconsistent Ilonian legal system—or even his own royal decree—could not.

But the sunset was taking its time tonight.

Paris Apollo stood out on the terrace that stretched alongside his private rooms, where so many of the Kings in Ilonian history had stood in their time, gazing out on the ocean beyond and all the islands that made the kingdom what it was.

He had changed out of the ceremonial robes and allowed himself some moments of much-needed solitude. He had reflected on the fact that his father had worn the very same historic robes in his time. And that the child even now tucked away in the lesser-used new wing of the palace would wear them someday, too. Troy would stand in the same hall and speak a great many of the same words to his people.

Paris Apollo found that the fact he was a father

was a concept far harder to grasp than the reality, two years old now, he was King.

And though he had planned almost every moment of this day down to the minutest details, from who was invited into his hall to exactly what he would say and how, he found that he'd anticipated Madelyn's arrival for the first supper they would share as an engaged couple almost more than all the rest.

It was that damned hunger inside of him that only seemed to sharpen with every moment he spent in her presence. It was that delirious need that he could recall only too well.

He could remember every sigh. Every touch. Every flicker of every flame that had danced between them. In them.

She hadn't disappointed him.

Madelyn hadn't changed from the gown she'd worn to the press conference, and he liked how it fit her. How it made her look like the very dream come true of a truly modern queen. Perfect for the kingdom, perfect for him.

He would have married her either way, naturally, so as to confer the necessary legitimacy upon his heir. He couldn't risk paying her off while he found another queen, not when the palace knew of her—giving any enemy with a DNA test a weapon to use against him in the future.

Even if he'd wanted to do such a thing, which he did not.

He didn't like the very idea of it.

What he did like was that Madelyn was a true commoner. A regular person, like so many of his subjects. And in time, the story of their separation—the massaged version, of course, filtered through the best royal spin there was—would make her even more dear to his people. For kings were necessarily icons. Relatable symbols, at best.

But Madelyn was a real person who had struggled and emerged victorious to take her place at his side, and he knew this would resonate with the kingdom. They would take to her and champion her, and this could only make his work easier.

Even the hint of scandal that would follow them, thanks to the existence of his child, could—if properly handled—make her all the more sympathetic to his people.

She really couldn't be more perfect.

He told himself he enjoyed what she brought to bear here, that was all. No *golden threads* required.

Paris Apollo even appreciated the way she barreled past his guards and into his rooms, as if he was a regular person, too. As if there was no need to stand on ceremony when they were alone. His parents never had, not when it was only them. He liked to imagine that they might look down upon him and—though they would feel sadness for the path of justice he had set himself upon and would not be impressed with the fact he'd allowed his heir to go astray for all these years, he knew—he flattered himself that they would approve of his choice of queen. Of a real woman, wholly unlike his usual conquests.

A man can only get so far with a cardboard cutout on his arm, King Aether had told him long ago, when Paris Apollo had been splashed all over some magazine with an actress whose name he barely knew.

But I like cardboard, Paris Apollo had replied, grinning. *It is so undemanding.*

That is not what a king wants in a queen, his father had said, peering at him with his usual concern. *I pray that you understand this before you find yourself trapped and miserable.*

Father, please. He had laughed then. For he'd believed he had so many decades left to keep laughing. *I am not capable of misery. Surely you know this.*

He had been wrong about that, too.

Now he was trapped, sure enough, though he did not intend to succumb to further misery on that score. He intended to enjoy it. And her. Surely that was the gift in all of this.

This time, he would enjoy her without losing his footing. This time, he knew better.

Paris Apollo could feel his body responding as she vented her spleen at him, reminding him in no uncertain terms that whatever else he was, he was a man first and foremost.

And she was…not a cardboard cutout.

She was real and she was his, like it or not. And he had already enjoyed Madelyn—too much, he would have said before her return. He saw no reason he should not enjoy her again. Surely that was the one thing their affair had been good for. It had shown him that he could indeed enjoy something a bit more substantial than cardboard.

That didn't mean he needed to lose the plot and start telling himself she was any kind of lodestone.

He'd already learned that lesson.

All of his plans were coming along swimmingly, he assured himself as the sky above them played with pinks and oranges and yellows and seemed in no hurry to surrender to the night.

Paris Apollo could relate.

"You're not even listening to me, are you?" Madelyn was demanding then, her hands on her hips and a distracting high color on her cheeks. "How dare you drag my son into this mess? In front of all those people and *cameras*? In this palace that isn't fit for children in the first place!"

"I was raised in this palace," he said very mildly. "Though I'm guessing you won't think that much of a draw."

He turned away from the view, leaning back on the rail so he could look at her instead. And also so he could practice that indolence that had once been such a part of him, because it no longer felt like second nature.

That impossible prettiness of Madelyn's seemed to infuse everything, even the dusk settling around her shoulders like a shawl.

That deep gold thread inside him pulled tight.

That longing in him was something more like a roar—

"Hear me," she bit out, and whatever he might have been about to do disappeared, lost somewhere in the way she held her hands on her hips, her censorious gray eyes fixed on him. "This will not happen. Troy is not a toy for you to play with. And I am not going to marry you. You might not remember what happened between us, but I do. Just as I remember exactly what was required to survive it. While caring for the child you didn't know existed until yesterday."

He didn't think she should remind him of that part. It wasn't wise. There was still that boiling well of fury inside him, and he didn't see it dissipating anytime soon—

But this was not the time for fury. Not directed at his future queen, at any rate.

Paris Apollo was sure there would be time enough for that in the years to come, when justice was served.

And it would be served. He intended to see to it personally.

"You will marry me," he corrected her, without any heat. Because there was no need to argue. She could fight this all the way down the aisle, for all he cared, and there was a part of him that hoped she would. A part that sat up and took notice of the building heat between them. "You and I will pledge our vows before the whole of my kingdom and the world. Our relationship will be all that is harmonious and aspirational, and if that is not true behind closed doors, it is of no matter. Lucky for me, the mother of my child is lovely. This is only to be expected, I grant you, but happily you are also a hard worker who isn't afraid of a struggle or two. You will be an enormous hit, I'm certain."

"I will not be a *hit*." Her chest was moving jaggedly, as if she was running a race while she stood still. He found himself mesmerized, remembering all the other ways he could make her breathe so heavily—until a frustrated sound brought his gaze to her face. "This isn't a game, Paris Apollo. This is my life. *My* life."

"You are the mother of my heir," he said mildly. Perhaps too mildly, the better to cover up all that wildfire inside of him. "By Ilonian law, your life is second to his, as is every other life in this kingdom save mine. It is a shamefully old-fashioned system, but there it is. A monarchy is all about its line of succession."

Madelyn swallowed, hard, a storm in that gray gaze of hers. He should not have found it so fascinating, when he knew that was part of what had ruined him the last time. "If you would like to be part of Troy's life, I won't deny you." She said that as if she was offering him a great concession. As if he had not already seen to it that there could be no such denials. "I realize now that I should have tried harder to involve you from the start."

"Do you think?"

And that was not quite as mild as the rest, he could admit.

Her gaze got darker. She shifted, dropping her hands from her hips. "I hope you understand that I was being completely honest when I said it never occurred to me to try. That is how different the two of us are. It was unimaginable to me that you would look down from all these palaces and thrones and *scepters* to take note of anything I might have been doing. *Lines of succession* were not something I considered at any point. But it turns out you *are* interested in Troy and I'm…delighted."

"Yes, Madelyn. Your delight is plain to see."

She ignored his dry tone. "I'm sure Troy will love getting to know his father. He's always wanted one. But none of these very reasonable decisions that you and I will undertake for his benefit make me a candidate to become your wife. Much less your *queen*."

He only watched her and waited.

And sure enough, she laughed out loud as if she'd made a joke. "I'm nobody's idea of a queen. The very idea is laughable. Absurd in every respect."

She laughed again to punctuate it.

"It is already done, my little Queen," Paris Apollo said softly. "Too many dies are already cast, I'm afraid. There are forces at play that make it impossible to allow any claim to throne to go unprotected. Both you and your son must remain under my protection."

"We wouldn't need your protection if you simply left the both of us alone."

"Perhaps you forget that I am not the one who found you." Paris Apollo lifted a shoulder, then dropped it, reminding himself as he did that there were eyes everywhere. Even here on this supposedly private terrace, and it would not do to tip his hand. His enemies must see him as the lazy Prince they'd imagined they could usurp. So he smiled. "If Angelique could find you, so, too, can my enemies. That would end differently, I think. And not in a way you would like."

"Is that a threat?"

He laughed. "Not from me."

"I will do anything to help Troy. *Obviously.* But that doesn't mean that I'm prepared to marry you. It's ridiculous that you would even ask."

"Madelyn." This time, it was a pleasure to keep his voice lazy, because he could hear the truth beneath. Steel and intent. And if he wasn't mistaken, so could she. "I did not ask."

Down on the far end of the terrace, his staff appeared and began setting out the evening meal. Paris Apollo pushed away from the rail, then gestured toward the table with exaggerated courtesy. Madelyn looked at him as if he was a lunatic, which he liked more than he should have, but she turned anyway. Then she stalked down the length of the terrace, a bristling sort of umbrage stamped over every inch of her.

Truly, each moment he spent with her, he enjoyed her more.

This time, he would enjoy her without losing his head. He would not be taken by surprise by the punch of her, for one thing. And for another, he was not the same man he'd been then.

There were too many scores he needed to settle to lose himself this time.

He took his place at the head of the table, waved his staff away, and waited. The table nearly groaned under the weight of the so-called *light supper* the kitchen had prepared to honor his return. Ilonia delicacies, mixed liberally with the usual Portuguese and Spanish influences. Yet he did not help himself. He continued to wait as Madelyn glared down at her plate, glared at the platters before her, and then, at last, glared at him.

"Was I bad in bed?" he asked idly. "Is that why you are so opposed to this union?"

And then he watched, delighted, as Madelyn... turned pink.

It was a creeping sort of pink, one that clearly came with heat. It rolled over her cheeks, down her neck, and then disappeared into the bodice of her dress. It made him highly interested in discovering exactly how far the tendrils of that pink heat reached.

If memory served, and he knew it served him far too well and too often, he could trace it all the way down to that sweet furrow between her legs.

She stared back at him, looking nothing short of mortified.

Paris Apollo felt his mouth curve as he helped himself to a fragrant heap of the roast pork stew that had always been his favorite, simmered for days in a spicy tomato mixture with a hint of cloves. "Not bad in bed, then, I gather. I am so relieved."

"I suppose I shouldn't be surprised that you're focused on sex," she said, angrily taking a seat at last, then glaring down at her empty plate. "As if such nonsense could possibly matter. We're not talking about a roll in the sheets, Paris Apollo. We're talking about a marriage. And I understand that marriage doesn't mean much to you. Maybe it's all dynasties and bloodlines and whatever else it is kings concern themselves with."

"No, that's it. There's certainly no governing or anything of that nature. That would be so boring."

She sniffed, still glaring and, sadly, much less pink. "The very idea of ruling anything once had you collapsing in laughter on the floor. Yet here we are. Do you really want me to believe that the most reckless, careless man I've ever met is suddenly deeply concerned with the legitimacy of a child? Because I don't believe it. I don't believe you care. And I know you don't care about me." She lifted her gaze then and when it settled on him, it made him feel something he couldn't understand at all. Small. When he had done nothing to earn that, save love her far too much and to his shame. "You never did. Why on earth would I shackle myself legally to that kind of misery?"

She still would not put food on her plate, so he did it for her. And if busying himself with the serving was a way to avoid addressing what she'd just said to him, well.

He was only a man, after all. As human as the rest.

Even though she looked at him as if his serving her the island's traditional food was a trick.

"Once again," he said when he sat back and shrugged as if he could not quite bring himself to care, "the dies are all cast.

"Then uncast them," she snapped. "Aren't you supposed to be the King here?"

Paris Apollo didn't respond to that. Because it was becoming clear that there was only one possible way to respond to this woman, and tonight was too soon to take things to that level. He had everything planned out. Every last thing that would lead him where he wanted to go, and he had stayed up all of last night factoring Madelyn Jones and her unexpected child into the equation.

His unexpected child.

He had decided that it could only benefit him to have an heir. Once he presented Troy to the kingdom, he would in many ways already have won the battle that loomed before him. His cousin Konos would lose a great many of his pet arguments then and there. Because it was easy to come up with reasons to discount Paris Apollo, the libertine or Paris Apollo, the tabloid staple. Paris Apollo, forever drowning in a particular kind of sin and scandal.

His cousin had made a cottage industry of whispering into this ear and that about how unlikely it was that the Paris Apollo everyone knew could ever step up to his responsibilities.

But the existence of a five-year-old heir and a queen to go with him was a *fait accompli*, and Paris Apollo knew it. The hint of scandal would surprise no one, but the end result would benefit him all the same.

Because he had gone up to the Hermitage a liability and come down settled and ready to rule. There was no way his treacherous cousin could have predicted such an outcome. Paris Apollo could not have predicted it himself.

He did not need Madelyn to be enthusiastic about her new role. This was Ilonia. He didn't even require her consent to marry her. All it required was his will.

But he did not think it necessary to clue her in to the finer points of Ilonian law.

Not yet.

He merely sat as the air turned soft around them. The pink in the sky was not unlike the heat that had suffused her skin, inching its way toward the horizon.

"This is ridiculous," Madelyn said crossly. "You truly expect me to sit here and share a meal with you? I thought it was above and beyond the call of duty to fly across the planet and inform you that you had a son. At no point did I ever indicate that I wanted to marry you."

"I have traveled quite a bit of the world and never found any bread I liked as much as Ilonian bread." Paris Apollo tried to sound helpful. He even smiled. "No need to take my word for it. There's some on your plate."

She shook her head, bristling again. "You don't even take this seriously. It's all one act or another."

He picked up his wineglass. "Is there acting? I do like a show."

"Yesterday you were storming around your stone tree house, grim and dangerous. Now you're lounging around at dinner tables, making remarks I have no doubt *you* think are entertaining. Which is the real you? Or is there nothing real to you at all?"

That was a bit more on point than he found comfortable. Especially when she was the only person alive who had ever managed to see beneath all of the masks he wore. He had spent years telling himself he had been mistaken. That he had lost himself in a pretty face, as many had done before him and would again.

It had not occurred to him that this woman would still be capable of seeing him clearly when no one else managed to do it.

This was most certainly not a part of his careful plans.

Paris Apollo swirled his wine around in his glass and eyed her over the top of it, ignoring the drumbeat inside him that seemed to take him over. "I am the King of Ilonia," he said simply enough, despite that low, insistent pounding that filled him up. "That's the only thing you need to know about me."

"I don't care if you're a king," she told him, her gray eyes solemn, and he hated that she could make that feel like some kind of conviction. When she held no high ground here. How could she imagine otherwise? "The only thing that matters to me about you at this point is that you're some kind of a father to Troy. That he is never hurt by his connection to you. That's it."

He thought of his own father, a man whose greatness had never been in doubt. For the young Aether had taken the throne when his own father had died unexpectedly, then made his youth and inexperience a selling point. He had invited his subjects to approach him with their concerns, reviving old traditions that brought his people to him. Like allowing anyone who wished to stand in line at the palace on certain days of the month for an audience with him. Where they could say anything they wished, and did. That had been his public face.

In private, Aether had been kind and fair, if perhaps too indulgent. But always possessed of a sense of humor. As if it was not a kingdom he carried, but a minor concern that paled next to his wife, his child. He had allowed Paris Apollo to feel as if, truly, his father was available to hear each and every one of his silly concerns when he was a child. He had not

Get up to 4
FREE FABULOUS BOOKS
You Love!

To thank you for being a loyal reader we'd like to send you up to 4 FREE BOOKS, absolutely free when you try the Harlequin Reader Service.

Just write "YES" on the Loyal Reader Voucher and we'll send you 2 free books from each series you choose and Free Mystery Gifts, altogether worth over $20.

Try **Harlequin® Desire** and get 2 books featuring the worlds of the American elite with juicy plot twists, delicious sensuality and intriguing scandal.

Try **Harlequin Presents® Larger-Print** and get 2 books featuring the glamourous lives of royals and billionaires in a world of exotic locations, where passion knows no bounds.

Or **TRY BOTH and get 2 books from each series!**

Your free books are completely free, even the shipping! If you continue with your subscription, you can look forward to curated monthly shipments of brand-new books from your selected series, always at a discount off the cover price! Plus you can cancel any time.

So don't miss out, return your Loyal Readers Voucher today to get your Free books.

Pam Powers

LOYAL READER
FREE BOOKS VOUCHER

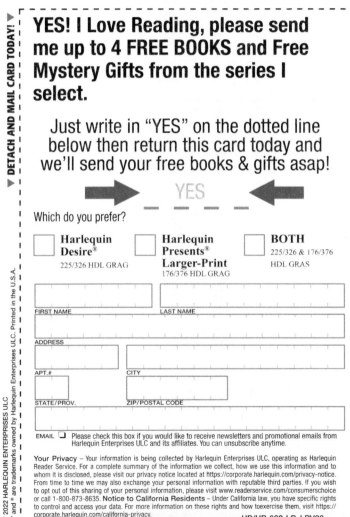

been shunted off to tutors and boarding schools like so many royal children were.

Paris Apollo hadn't had the faintest idea how unique this was until he met the children of other wealthy men—whether royal or not—at Cambridge.

"I intend to be an excellent father to my son," he said, because he didn't know how to put his admiration for his own father into words. Not when he was still too focused on dispensing the necessary justice for Aether's untimely death. "One way or another."

"Do you really." That came out a challenge, not a question. "When you couldn't even take it upon yourself to meet him. After dragging him all the way here just so you could use him to keep me in line."

She pushed back from the table and stood in a sudden clamor of the chair against the stone and her own obvious temper. Paris Apollo found himself rising as well, tracking her as she whirled around and stomped toward the doors that led into the public rooms of his apartment, though she did not go inside.

Instead, she turned back to face him. The last of the sun was still clinging to the horizon, a deep glow in the distance. The night air around them was cool, and the terrace was lit all around with the great hanging lanterns his people favored.

The only storm here tonight was in Madelyn's gaze.

And that drumbeat deep inside him, low in his sex, as if the only hunger he would ever feel was for her.

Always for her.

As if she hadn't ruined him long ago.

"This is real life." And though her voice was quiet, he could hear the undercurrent in it that told him how deeply her feelings ran. But then, so did his. "It is Troy's real life, Paris Apollo. This isn't whatever game you think you're playing with us. His life matters more than whatever dies are cast or whatever court intrigue is happening here. He has nothing to do with any of it."

"That is where you are wrong," Paris Apollo replied, and he sounded almost regretful, there in the gathering night. Though he was not. There was nothing here to regret. Not when there was vengeance waiting in the coming night and, here between them, this same, simmering desire that had been there from the start. "You have had five years to enjoy being the sun and the moon and the whole of the stars for that little boy. *That* was not real life, Madelyn. That was only ever a fantasy, and had I known sooner, it would not have lasted as long as it did. Because for all your talk of fairy tales and the things that should have occurred yet conveniently slipped your mind, I remain the King of Ilonia."

"You keep expecting that to impress me—" she began hotly.

"I am stating a fact. You keep glossing over it. My son is the Crown Prince whether you marry me or not, because he is my heir apparent by virtue of his blood and his very existence."

"Wonderful." Her tone was no less spicy then. "Even less reason to get married."

He allowed himself a long-suffering sigh. "You marrying me gives the whole enterprise a gloss of respectability, of tradition. And ensures that no other potential heir could claim they have more right to the throne than Troy does in the event of my death."

She scowled. "I don't *want* him to have anything to do with your stupid throne."

Paris Apollo only smiled, ignoring that. "It is also not lost on me that while my people were remarkably tolerant of my behavior as a single man, as a mere prince to my parents' King and Queen, things are different now." More different than he wished, or could reconcile himself with, but that was a separate conversation entirely—and one he did not intend to have. Not with a woman who looked pink and hot and *his*. "It will serve all of us better if I present myself to them now as a man grown. Settled and steady, with the wife and child to prove it."

Madelyn surged toward him, her scowl something like ferocious. Then, to his utter astonishment, she extended one finger and poked it into the center of his chest.

Once, then again.

He peered down at his own chest in amazement.

And not only because she dared touch him, as the King. But because she dared touch him as a man when she claimed to remember exactly how it had always been between them.

A conflagration from the very start.

He was surprised the ancient city of Cambridge still stood.

But she did not stop. She seemed utterly heedless, and that only made the current of need in him pull tauter. "You have not mentioned one thing that isn't about you. Not one small thing that isn't entirely centered on *you, you, you*. And yet you think I should marry you? So I can take up what appears to be a kingdom-wide delusion that you are anything but a narcissistic disaster? Why would anyone do that? Why *should* I?"

"I flatter myself that there are some compensations," Paris Apollo found himself saying, in a kind of low growl that hardly sounded like him at all.

Madelyn scoffed. "Name one."

He wrapped his hand around that pointing finger of hers. He jerked her into his arms.

Then he bent his head and kissed her.

And her taste slammed into him like a sledgehammer. The instant heat of her mouth, the way her lips fit his.

He kissed her deeper, wilder, the demonstration he'd intended lost almost before he started because all he could think to do was pull her closer, kiss her deeper.

And as he did, he stopped pretending.

Because he'd still been telling himself stories, hadn't he? About his ruin, but always tempered by the years in between...

But her taste was the truth.

It was his true ruin and always had been.

He had been stunned by this woman at first sight, in a grotty little pub he'd long since forgotten why he'd ever gone to in the first place. And it had been overwhelming and intense, just like this, from that very first instant.

It had been like a searing wildfire summer after a long, cold, stricken winter that had gone on forever.

It still was.

Paris Apollo had always been a man of enthusiastic appetites, but she had made him feel as if he was no more than an untried boy, turned inside out for the very first time.

She had become his obsession.

And he had lost himself in her. Completely.

His friends had despaired of him.

How could he blame them? He hadn't. He had become a stranger—not that he'd cared.

Because she was his earthquake, a pretty little seismic disaster, and Paris Apollo had been perfectly prepared to walk away from his carefree life forever. For her.

He had thought Annabel was lying to him about Madelyn. He'd told her so.

Then by all means, wait to see how quickly she calls you, his friend had invited him. *If you're more to her than a memento of her little trip, she should keep in touch, shouldn't she?*

He had never told anyone how long it had taken

him to stop hoping she would call. How many years it had been before he'd stopped reacting to any unknown number even though, after she'd gone, Paris Apollo had committed himself wholeheartedly to oblivion in all forms. He had never spoken Madelyn's name again.

And now he understood that the deepest lies he'd ever told had been to himself.

Each and every time he'd pretended that he could handle this.

He wrenched his mouth from hers and stood back, appalled.

She was the very last woman he should have permitted to come here, much less become his queen. She was the worst possible choice to be the mother of his child. Madelyn Jones was a distraction. A driving, consuming obsession when he could ill afford any such thing.

The only thing he needed to concentrate on—or would allow himself to concentrate on—was making certain his parents were avenged. That justice was finally served.

Something he could not do with this woman clouding his judgment.

He set her apart from him and saw far too much in those wide gray eyes of hers. All that heat. All that longing. All the memories of the ways their bodies had come together. The pleasure he had taken in her innocence, a gift she had bestowed upon him so sweetly that it made his bones ache to recall it now, damn her—

"You look like you've seen a ghost." Her voice was thick. That did not help.

Because she was the only ghost who had ever haunted him, and he'd gone to great lengths to excise her. And he'd told himself so many lies about his plans and how this would work between them now that he was a new man—

But one kiss made it clear that where she was concerned, he would always be that same poor fool who had been so besotted with her in Cambridge.

No matter who might have died in the interim.

"It turns out I do remember you after all," he bit out.

Because he had to say something.

He had to order himself to let go of her shoulders. To step back and put some space between them.

"My condolences," she threw at him, temper kindling in that gaze of hers. "I'm sorry that remembering the mother of your child distresses you."

"It will make no difference," Paris Apollo gritted out, though he felt as if every word cursed them both. "You and I *will* marry, Madelyn. There will be no divorce. There is no possible way out. So perhaps it is both of us who require condolences."

And later, after she'd whirled around and rushed off, he stared out at his city arrayed below him. The way he'd dreamed of doing these last two years. The dark came in at last, inky and thick, and he welcomed it.

He exulted in it.

For it was time to put the skills he'd taught himself at the Hermitage to good use at last. It was time to enact his vengeance.

But he found he stayed there on that terrace—thinking of her mouth beneath his and the memories he wished he really had blocked from his own head—for much longer than he should have. When there was the whole of the island to reacquaint himself with under cover of night.

No one would expect the King to tread in the places Paris Apollo intended to go in search of justice for his parents.

And that was precisely what he was counting on.

Ghosts or no ghosts.

CHAPTER SIX

MADELYN STAGGERED OUT into the hallway and then tried to walk along it as if everything was fine. As if she was *fine* when she very much doubted that she would ever be anything like *fine* again...

Yet she was overly aware that people could see her, from the unobtrusive but watchful staff to the guards stationed at their usual intervals.

She really, truly, did not wish any of them to notice that she was on fire.

When surely the blaze inside of her and all over her could be seen from space.

So she walked as quickly as she could without seeming to run. She tried to look composed and at ease, though glimpses in the various shiny, reflective surfaces that were all over the palace made her doubt she was fooling anyone. And when she finally made it out of the busy part of the palace, she let herself slow down. And breathe a little.

That only made it worse.

She was hungry because she hadn't eaten a bite on that terrace. She was irritated because...

Well. *Because everything.*

There was a large part of her that wanted to pretend this hadn't happened, the way she'd been pretending so much hadn't happened, so she could run back to her rooms, cuddle with Troy, and act as if nothing had changed.

But everything had changed.

And the worst part of this was that she could no longer pretend otherwise.

Because she could feel it inside of her. All over her, this impossible fire. This maddening blaze of heat and longing, this ache that was the reason all of this had happened in the first place.

Because she had looked up from her life, seen him, and nothing had been the same since.

She wasn't sure how she'd managed to forget all of this.

Particularly the wildfire seduction of his kiss.

One taste of Paris Apollo and she would have done anything. She had.

Her parents weren't the only ones who had lost a little faith in her and her decisions.

The difference being, you know that Troy is worth it, a voice in her chimed in at once, the way it always did. Because that was what mattered. At times he had been the only thing that mattered to her.

Paris Apollo couldn't change that.

Madelyn staggered down one hallway. Then, feeling claustrophobic—even though there was nothing the least bit confining about these wide marble halls and arched ceilings—she saw a set of doors that led outside and pushed her way through them.

There was still light far off in the sky, a hint of daylight somewhere else. But she didn't have it in her to wish she was following the light, because the dark was pushing in and it felt soothing.

Just for a moment, Madelyn thought, she could take a minute to soothe herself.

She felt guilty because Troy was here and for once she didn't have to rush off to pick up a shift. She could spend all the time with him she liked, and she should. She would. Still, with only a backward glance at the looming palace, Madelyn set off across the path that opened up in front of her and found herself in the gardens.

She could smell sweet flowers in the night—night blooming-jasmine, bright mimosa, and a lingering note of deep green mixed through with a bit of salt from the sea. The pathways were lit by the same warm lanterns she'd noticed against her will up on that terrace with Paris Apollo. She had seen the gardens from her windows earlier, but in the dark they took on an air of mystery. Romance. It was the buttery light of the lanterns—

Madelyn ordered herself to stop thinking about pretty lanterns. Wasn't that how she'd gotten herself into this mess? She'd spent too much time thinking about things she shouldn't have. Whole years wrapped up in tiny concerns, like how to get a better serving job at a better restaurant in a better resort. When all along she should have been focused on what was happening here in these islands.

Of course she'd looked them up. She wasn't *that* naive. But tales of isolated islands and hereditary monarchies in the high seas seemed like bedtime stories when there were so many less fantastical details to focus on every day. Like bills. Preschool. All the marvelous and stultifying things about parenting, many in the same stretch of five minutes.

She obviously should have been paying attention to what Paris Apollo and his parents were doing this whole time so she could have reacted quicker. So she could have *done something*.

So she could have avoided forever the truths she learned about herself tonight.

After all this time. After all that had happened. After the truth she'd had to face at the top of those stairs in Cambridge, and many harder truths afterward. When her parents had turned her away. When she'd given birth all alone. When she'd stayed up in the night, nursing Troy and sobbing as much because of the ways her body was ravaged as because she was so tired and so uncertain how she was going to make it to morning…

Sometimes it hadn't been clear how she was going to make it to the next hour.

And all of that had simply…gone up in flames tonight.

All it had taken was a kiss.

Madelyn despaired of herself.

But that was nothing new. And the only cure for this feeling that she'd ever found was walking. That was all she'd done when she'd come home from England that August. She'd gone to her classes and, in between them, walked around the city. Up and down the famous hills, in and around the marinas and the parks. Across the Golden Gate Bridge and back. Not that walking solved a thing, she thought now as she made her way down one garden path, then up another, noting the way the lantern light caught the long skirt of her dress. The way the pools of light seemed to urge her on.

But solved or not, she felt calmer for it. So she kept walking.

She had no idea how much time had passed when she found herself at the farthest edge of the garden. For a while, she followed the stone wall there, gazing over it and down across the sweep of the city, gleaming and sparkling in the dark. She couldn't see the ocean, but there was no mistaking where it was. That inky black, there on the edges of everything.

Hovering. Waiting. Lurking, even.

But no matter how many dramatic words she conjured up to describe it, Madelyn still found something about its presence peaceful. As if, no matter the petty concerns of a woman with a child high up on a hilltop, the ocean would endure.

Maybe she would, too.

Madelyn blew out a shaky breath and turned

around, finally looking back up at the palace as it sat there above her in all its splendor.

And maybe she hadn't slept as well last night as she would have liked. Maybe being stranded in a stone hermitage and then let loose on the grounds of an actual palace made her a bit fanciful.

But she couldn't help thinking that the palace represented Paris Apollo a little too well. It was stunning. Beautiful. It almost hurt to look upon it in all of its glowing glory as she stood here in the dark.

She told herself it was less about the light that shone from it—and the man who personified this place to her—and more about the unchangeable traditions and centuries of autocratic rule that it represented. Traditions she was now swept up in, like it or not.

Madelyn let out a short little laugh at that and figured she might as well head back inside, if she'd managed to amuse herself.

That was certainly better than the frazzled burnt-to-a-crisp way she'd felt when she staggered out of Paris Apollo's rooms. She pressed her fingers to her lips as she walked, telling herself they felt completely normal now.

Just as she told herself she couldn't taste him on her tongue.

She took a long, lazy loop through the garden, keeping to the hedges and edges that kept her in the overgrown parts with very little light. There was even a bench set in the darkest stretch, shielded from the palace's light by a copse of pines. Madelyn wondered who had placed it *just so*, almost certainly to allow whoever sat here to look out over the ocean and up at the stars without any interference. On another night, when she didn't need to walk and didn't have that clamoring inside her that told her she needed to get back to Troy, she thought she might sit awhile. Breathe it all in, deep. Then let herself feel as if she was tumbling out into the stars herself.

Not that you intend to spend any amount of time here, she reminded herself sternly. *Because there's no possible way you're going to become his queen, no matter what he might think.*

It was funny, though, that there was some kind of quivering, deep inside her, that suggested otherwise.

And later, she was tucked back up in the apartment she been given. She was lying in a bed that was bigger than the entirety of her bedroom at home, with Troy cuddled up against her side, his thumb in his mouth as if he was still a baby. And she found herself staring up at the colorful ceiling and wondering about the other thing she'd seen out there.

Not the stars. Not the great black expanse of the sea.

But the shadows that had seemed to move in her peripheral vision.

Shadows that she could have sworn took the shape of Paris Apollo, but dressed as he'd been in the Hermitage yesterday. In those black assassin-type clothes that clung close to his body and made him look like some kind of action hero instead of a pampered, spoiled king.

"You need to sleep," she whispered to herself, there in the dark. She closed her eyes. She held her son's body—hot and faintly flushed because Troy slept as hard as he played—close to hers the way she often did when he crawled into her bed to cuddle up with her.

But there was no relief to be found.

Only fire.

The palace wedding machine lurched into gear, starting early the next morning. Squadrons of smartly dressed and impeccably cheerful staff members descended upon her in shifts, all of them insisting that *everyone*—by which, they meant Madelyn—needed to pitch in to get her ready for the role they'd decided she must take.

But Madelyn refused to play along.

No matter how brightly her attendants told her that she needed to turn up at this time or in this place, she didn't. Instead, she and her aunt took Troy for long walks when it was sunny, out on the rambling palace grounds, which she was sure had to be bigger than her favorite park in San Francisco. When the weather was less cooperative, they raced up and down the grand marble halls, as if the palace was no more than a playground.

And in many ways, it was better than any playground they had ever been to before. Because the palace not only had hallways stuffed full of antiquities, but many of them also featured suits of armor and sharp weapons that five-year-old Troy found fascinating. It also had its own labyrinth, on the lowest level, where there must have once been dungeons.

Troy was particularly interested in the possibility of dungeons. He'd turned five and become bloodthirsty. Something Madelyn imagined she would have to deal with if it continued a decade from now.

But right now he was five. And when he wasn't being the little monster that could come out sometimes, she found him perfect and angelic and adorable, particularly when he shrieked a little, giggled, and pronounced some tale of ancient torture *cool*.

Instead of attending the many meetings that were presented to her on carefully filled out daily agendas she didn't read, Madelyn spent time with her kid. Something she never got to do as much as she wanted at home. And when he napped or wanted to play with his great-aunt Corrine instead, she read the papers. There were no physical papers in the palace, she quickly found, but despite all indications to the contrary, they were not actually living in the dark ages. Palace or no palace.

She had a phone. And there were a number of libraries in this sprawling place, so it was easy enough to find herself a cozy nook and catch up on the papers she was pretty sure were probably being deliberately withheld from her.

And with good reason because her face was everywhere.

Madelyn studied them all and couldn't understand how anyone could look at these photographs of her and not realize that she'd been anything but a blushing, delighted fiancée up on that dais. Paris Apollo looked powerful and certain, as a king should. Especially when he'd lifted her hand to his mouth, then kissed her as if he was branding her.

Property of the Kingdom of Ilonia. As surely as if he'd stamped it on her forehead.

Madelyn thought it was obvious that she was stunned. Out of her depth. If not actively opposed.

Yet most of the papers claimed that it was all swooningly romantic.

As if that wasn't enough, a great many of them spent the days since the announcement doing deep dives on Madelyn's life, trying to make sense of what the palace had called the *period of contemplation* she had undergone, suggesting that she'd been debating if she wanted to live her life in the public eye—and had possibly also wanted to keep Troy hidden from the vultures. They were just vague enough. They made it all seem honorable. They even suggested that the worst of the King's excesses had been him attempting to handle her laudable step back from the notion of royal life, the better to protect their son.

The implication was that she had been willing to

sacrifice true love to protect her child, while *he* had been willing to give up both his child and his beloved to keep them safe, if that was what she wished.

They both sounded like idiots, in Madelyn's opinion, but the world seemed to eat it all up.

Meanwhile, the papers unearthed photographs of her that she had to stare at furiously, trying to place them. One from some play she was in way back in high school. Another that made her look ferocious, clearly on her way out of work one night.

One of her on the front porch of her parents' house that could only have been sent in by a childhood friend.

But even stranger than the unearthed photography was the appearance of people like the nasty Lady Annabel, who rose from the darkest part of Madelyn's memories to splash herself all over every available surface she could find. Entertainment shows. Blog posts. Tabloids in all forms. In each and every one, Annabel gave authoritative statements regarding not only her close personal knowledge of Paris Apollo—*Wink-wink, yes, darlings,* that *kind of knowledge... the man is a tiger*—but also her own reflections on how she, personally, had brought Paris Apollo and the most unlikely girl in the world together all those years ago in Cambridge. She even made up bald-faced lies about what had gone on between them since.

Casting herself as the matchmaking center of it all, of course.

Madelyn told herself she really shouldn't be surprised that Annabel was as repulsive as ever. She wasn't. What surprised her was that she couldn't bring herself to look away.

Even though she had no intention of staying in Ilonia. She certainly had no interest in becoming Paris Apollo's queen. *Marrying him*, for God's sake. It was nothing but idle interest that led her to look through the Ilonian papers, too. They were so helpfully translated into three languages.

She found herself in all of them. And also, always lower down in whatever was going on at the palace, articles discussing a rash of strange, vigilante-type justice on the islands. Or so the papers assumed, as every morning the central police station reported that certain well-known miscreants were delivered to them. Not the general thieves and addicts and scam artists who cluttered up the seedier parts of the harbor. But the kind of villains who had troubling connections to Ilonian aristocrats.

One reporter went so far as to say it almost seemed to her as if a net was closing. Around what, no one dared say.

But the fact that the former King and Queen had died in an accident at sea that everyone whispered was far more than an accident always seemed to be the undercurrent in every article that Madelyn read.

And so every night, Madelyn lay in that bed of hers in the new wing of the palace, where the pa-

parazzi were never allowed, and thought of the things she'd seen in the shadows.

Of Paris Apollo, dressed to disappear, scaling walls and taking himself off into the dark.

Yet in the daylight, as his people tried to apply more and more pressure to her, she found what occupied her thoughts the most was the undeniable fact that he had yet to introduce himself to Troy.

He had not even tried.

"How long are we going to be on vacation?" Troy asked her over breakfast one morning. "I miss home."

Madelyn and her aunt exchanged glances. "I miss home, too," Madelyn said calmly. "But I think it's fun here. Don't you?"

"Everybody talks about the King," her son told her, his gray-green eyes big and wide and so innocent it made Madelyn want to wrap him up in cotton wool and protect him forever. "But I never get to see him."

That lodged itself like a bullet beneath her ribs. Every time she breathed, it hurt. Every time she even thought about moving, it was like that very same spot got irritated and inflamed her whole body.

And so, when his people cornered her on her way to the library later that day, she lost her cool.

"Are these the orders of the King?" she demanded, staring coolly at the man who was always chasing her down with these details, dressed in smooth black and forever aiming that obsequious smile her way.

It only made him seem all the more condescending. "You've been sent here on his behalf, I expect?"

"Of course, madam," the man said in his fine, overly cultured voice. "Nothing is done in the palace without the King's express direction."

"Then let me give you an *express direction* of my own," she replied. She knew it was important that she not speak from the place where that bullet was lodged. She knew that it was necessary she seem as unbothered and unaffected as she assumed Paris Apollo was. But it was so much harder than she expected. "Your king has a child. A child who has never met his father. Why on earth would I succumb to any of his demands when he can't do his own child the most basic of courtesies *and meet him*?"

"It is not ours to question the will—" tutted the man.

"Maybe it's not yours," Madelyn interrupted him fiercely, that bullet wound throbbing inside her. "But it's certainly mine. Especially where my son is concerned. I don't want to hear another word about what Paris Apollo wants. Not until he stops talking about responsibilities for others and meets his."

She didn't wait for the man to answer. She brushed past him and stormed off down the hall, carried along on the force and power of her own self-righteous indignation, not caring at all if the entire palace knew exactly how furious she was.

And part of her was braced for Paris Apollo's immediate appearance, but he didn't come. Not that day.

Not the next. And it wasn't until they were creeping toward the end of their second week of life in the Ilonian Palace that she accepted the fact that he... wasn't going to come. It didn't matter that he'd sent his doctors that first day to take the blood samples that would prove, beyond a shadow of a doubt, what Madelyn had always known to be true. It didn't matter that he'd brought Troy here in the first place.

She couldn't begin to imagine the reason he was avoiding his *heir apparent*, especially not when she'd sat on that terrace and listened to him talk so callously of all the ways he could use Troy's existence for his own ends. But he had no intention of meeting his own child. He'd made that patently clear.

He proved, once again, that he was exactly who Annabel had said he was. The man who broke his toys.

Madelyn told herself she didn't care. She'd never expected them to meet in the first place. She would be perfectly happy to take Troy right back home.

Even if, deep down, there was a part of her that thought that actually, the fact she'd never tried to meet *her* responsibilities where notifying Paris Apollo was concerned was nothing to be proud of, either.

And so in the end, some days later, she was completely unprepared to come around a corner in the gardens, laughing at Troy's antics, and come face-to-face with Paris Apollo.

"Hey!" Troy cried happily. "You're the King!"

"I am," Paris Apollo replied. And he wasn't dressed in suspicious black today. He wore black, yes, but not the sort of black that anyone would use to scale a wall. Today, it was a dark suit with quiet touches that lent him that air of offhanded elegance. He looked darkly blond and beautiful, the way an archangel might, and Madelyn had to restrain herself from slapping her own face at that idiocy. "I hear your name is Troy."

"I am Troy," Troy replied, in that overtly serious way he sometimes had. He blinked. "What's it like to be a king? Did that crown hurt your head? Do you get to play with it whenever you want?"

He continued to ask questions, one blending into the next. And Madelyn braced herself for Paris Apollo, who she couldn't imagine in the company of the child, turning away. Looking at his own child with disdain—and she was ready for that. She would fly at him, she told herself. She would snatch Troy up, and run, and scale the wall herself. She would never let him treat her son badly. Not even for a moment—

But he didn't do any of that.

Instead, she watched as King Paris Apollo, who looked like an archangel but was not one, crouched so he could put himself at Troy's eye level.

As Madelyn held her breath, he then proceeded to answer each and every one of Troy's questions as if he had nothing else to do with his time and never would.

"Are you my dad?" Troy asked him at the end of all these questions. It was matter-of-fact. He looked at Madelyn, then back at Paris Apollo. "I heard the maids talking and they said you are. But I didn't want to ask my mom. She always gets sad when I ask her about my dad."

Madelyn discovered, then, that there were so many new and different kinds of heartbreak. So many more variations on that theme.

One was learning, like this, that her son had seen that sadness she'd been so sure she'd hidden well.

And another was this one that she hadn't known she held so dear in her heart, coming true at last.

Paris Apollo looked up at Madelyn, his expression as serious as his son's. It hit her hard. Then he looked back at Troy, man-to-man.

"I am your dad," he said, in the same matter-of-fact way. "And I've been waiting a long time to meet you."

CHAPTER SEVEN

THAT NIGHT, PARIS APOLLO summoned Madelyn to his chambers.

The weeks back in the palace had gone exactly to plan. He had gone over every possible detail, or so he'd imagined up there in the Hermitage, but he'd also allowed for the possibility that there would be unforeseen complications.

So far his predictions had been on point. Every night, he took to the streets exactly as intended. He hunted down all the nasty little far-reaching tendrils of his cousin's disease, rounding them up and dropping them off to make certain they could do no more damage to the kingdom.

And just in case there was any confusion, he left a list of their transgressions pinned to their chests.

Are you crazy? one of them had asked only last night. *You think there were scandals before? Women and such? What do you think* this *will look like when it hits the news?*

Who do you suppose will believe you? Paris

Apollo had replied with a grim sort of satisfaction. *I can't think of a better way to announce that you might be a delusional drug addict than to shoot off your mouth about this fantasy you have that the King of Ilonia is tramping about the streets at night, consorting with the likes of you.*

Sure enough, there hadn't been so much as a whisper of his involvement. Just as he'd planned.

Things had been going so swimmingly in that department, and with all his plans, that he'd thought it was finally time to do something about the child.

His child. His *son.*

But he hadn't let himself dwell too much on the boy. He couldn't. Not until it was time.

Not until he had done *something* to avenge his parents. That might not make him feel that he deserved this new family that had been thrust upon him, here in the ashes of the old family he had not treated as he should have. But it would be something.

It would be *something.*

His man had faithfully reported back what Madelyn had said about the King's responsibilities as a father. Paris Apollo could even admit, privately, that she'd had a point. Because he had not needed the blood test the palace's legal ministers had insisted upon when he ordered them to change his will and begin the official process of naming Troy his son and heir. He would have had to be a blind man to miss the fact that the child was made in his image. It was like looking through a time warp.

But, of course, that wasn't the same thing as actually interacting with the child.

Troy, he had told himself stoutly, day after day. Not *the child*. Not *the boy*. Not *the heir*.

The boy's name was Troy. He needed to use it. He needed to engrave it on his bones because surely that was what fatherhood was.

That was how it had always felt to be Aether's son.

Paris Apollo had prepared for a great many things, up there in his stone retreat for those two years of grief. How to track down each and every person he had determined had a hand in his parents' deaths. How to circle his cousin carefully so that his revenge might be as cold as possible. He had considered a thousand possibilities of the way things could go depending on an ever-shifting number of factors. He'd conditioned his body. He'd sharpened his skills in a hundred different ways to make himself ready.

He'd been so certain he was ready for everything and anything he might face when he came down that mountain and took his throne in full.

But he hadn't been prepared for Troy.

He hadn't been ready for the tidal wave of emotion that had knocked him this way and that in the gardens today. He hadn't been prepared for what it would feel like to have a whole conversation with his own child. *His child.* To answer Troy's questions, ask his own, and find himself fascinated by the way the child's young mind worked.

He hadn't been ready for how it would feel to

study his son's small body and see things that he knew were his. *His* nose. *His* face. The shape of his shoulders, the jut of his chin, that Paris Apollo knew, in time, would resemble his own.

That night in the Hermitage, he had been shocked at the news that he had a son. He had been unimpressed by Madelyn's suggestion that it had never crossed her mind to let him know he was a father. But he had channeled all that into action. He had been able to find a cool, rational distance from the issue and had seen exactly how this revelation could best benefit him and his reign.

He had commended himself on accepting such a huge plot twist with equanimity. That night, he hadn't slept at all. He had stood there watching the dawn break over the islands from his windows, congratulating himself. For he had come into the Hermitage a broken son who knew only how to be a lackluster prince, but he would leave those stones a king and a father, able to handle anything that was thrown his way.

But today he could not access that sense of composure.

Today Paris Apollo felt nothing but the deepest betrayal. It felt like a howling thing within him, dark and wild—and he rather thought she knew it.

Because Madelyn didn't make him seek her out tonight. He'd been perhaps a little too ready for that. There was something stirring in his blood, some kind of predatory fury—

In truth, he wanted it. He *wanted* the excuse to stalk through the halls of this palace, find her, and call her to account.

Any way he could. Every way he could.

Instead, Madelyn not only appeared a good five minutes before the appointed hour, but she also came dressed appropriately for a dinner with a king. When he was all too aware that she had been shirking such considerations the whole time she'd been here, deliberately defying his staff's requests as if that might save her from the fate that awaited her.

Nothing can, he thought now, with no little pleasure. *There is no escape.*

They would wed in a couple of short weeks. And that was that, for Ilonian monarchs did not divorce. It was only a matter of coming to terms with the inevitable, Paris Apollo thought.

She would have a great many years before her to practice.

He found her waiting for him out on that same terrace, though this time, her hands were not already on her hips. She was not glaring at him. This time, he found her staring off over the railing, into the gardens and the city and sea beyond, a troubled look on her face.

She was not starting off on the offensive tonight, then. That beast in him roared its approval. Because he certainly was.

"So you are capable of behaving like the future Queen of this country after all." He belted that out and then watched the way she stiffened. Though she did not turn to face him. "My staff report that you are more often found dressed like our son. Jeans and a T-shirt, rolling about in the dirt or hiding from your duties in the libraries."

"Is this really what you wish to speak about tonight, Paris Apollo?" Madelyn's voice was mild, but he wasn't fooled. Not tonight. Tonight, he felt seared straight through with a kind of clarity he wasn't sure he'd ever had before. Not where she was concerned. "This is the only topic you can think of? Are you certain?"

"Do you dare to attempt to call me out?" He roamed toward her, hungering to put his hands on her, but he did not. He did not dare. Not yet. "After your own sins? Or have you forgotten?"

"I never claimed I had a poor memory." She turned to face him, then, and he disliked how easily she could render him…undone. With only a look. A pitying sort of look now, as if she alone could see the truth of him. "I believe that's you."

And there were too many parts of this that Paris Apollo did not wish to look at head-on. He had tried, these past couple of weeks, to set aside the things that kiss had made so clear to him.

Like the ways he had deceived himself. Like his own cowardice. That he had been so willing to act the way he had. That he had tried so hard to pretend she was nothing to him. That he had dedicated himself to the attempt to tamp it all down, hide it away, as if it had never been.

When he'd pretended he didn't know her, and not for any reason but the most petty and unworthy: he had hoped it would hurt her.

His parents would not have approved. He knew that.

Are you angry at her? asked a voice in Paris Apollo's head that sounded far too much like his mother's. Cool, serene, and yet unflinching. *Or are you angry with yourself?*

But he knew the answer to that too well because he didn't *want* to answer it.

"How could you keep him from me?" he demanded, though he kept his voice a low growl. "How could you pretend to yourself that I would not care?"

He expected she might flinch at that, but if anything, she stood taller. And her gaze remained as it ever was, direct and steady. "You didn't care about me. Why would it cross my mind that you'd care if I had a child? I've already apologized, Paris Apollo. And I'm sorry that you can't accept my thinking on this. But that doesn't mean I'm lying about it."

"And do you truly believe that I will ever let you leave my sight again?" he continued as if she hadn't spoken, his voice a dangerous throb. "Do you imagine for one moment that now, having finally met the son you kept from me, I would ever let him go again?"

He watched that move through her and was glad

of it. Glad that she might feel some small portion of what he did.

"I told you that I'm happy to share custody with you," she said very carefully. And perhaps not as steadily as before.

"Do you imagine your happiness signifies?"

"I saw how you were with him today. It was…" And he thought that the way she swallowed then— too hard, too loud—showed that she was as distressed by this as he was. But he didn't wish to know that. He did not wish to see it. "I can't change the past."

"Perhaps not. But understand that I own your future, Madelyn. Because you owe me. And I have no compunction whatsoever in taking what I am owed."

"What *you* are owed." She let out a sharp laugh at that. Her gray eyes flashed hot. "You are unbelievable. I don't *owe* you anything."

And something in him—that roaring beast— stilled in anticipation.

Because this was the fight he had longed for. He could see it all over her, in the way her whole body vibrated as she pushed away from the rail and stepped toward him. The way she scowled at him, temper making her flush bright, as if she wanted nothing more than to get into the fight they both were spoiling for.

Neither did he.

"Believe it," he suggested. Not kindly.

"I am Troy's mother. I decide what happens to him

and who gets to see him, not you. You're not even on his birth certificate. You have no rights here that I don't grant you."

"You forget who you are speaking to," he shot back with a soft menace. "You are on Ilonian soil, where it has already been decided that Troy is my heir. Your wishes matter as much as a foreign birth certificate does, which is to say—not at all." She started to argue, but he slashed a hand through the air, cutting her off. "I have been gentle with you, Madelyn, but you must know by now that I am the law here. Whatever *I* wish. Whatever *I* command. You have the standing I grant you as a courtesy, but nothing more."

Something in her seemed to ignite. She closed the distance between them, once again making the foolish mistake of touching him. This time not with a finger, but a whole palm. She slapped it into the center of his chest and then looked faintly surprised, as if she'd actually believed she could toss him back across his own terrace.

Paris Apollo did not move even the faintest centimeter.

"I want nothing from you," she threw at him. "Not one thing."

"You're a liar."

"Does that make you feel better? To imagine that you still have the same hold over me that you did when I was so foolish and so naive and actually believed that you were the man you pretend to be?"

Madelyn let out high, strange sort of laugh that he understood was meant to function much as that slap had. And he could feel the force of it. It was far more effective than a hand on his chest.

But then, he had a use for that, too. He reached up and covered her hand with his.

And he could feel that fire again, the great wave of it. An impossible blaze, sweeping through him, through her.

As if, together, they set the night on fire, making their own lightning storm.

"You're the one who dragged me here," she seethed at him. "I want nothing to do with you and nothing from you, ever."

"Except this, Madelyn," he growled, using his hand to jerk her off-balance and into his arms, splayed out over the wall of his chest. "Except *this*."

And this time, when he brought his mouth down on hers, it was a reckoning.

It was condemnation, accusation, and far and above either, an immolation.

Paris Apollo felt that same explosion in both of them, and then everything was fire.

The night. The two of them.

And he knew that what was required here was strategy. Tactical prowess. But he had none of that to give, not with her taste in his mouth, changing him. Recreating him.

He had only this heat. This need.

And the mad longing that roared through him, obliterating everything else.

He kissed her and he kissed her, shoving his hands into the intricate design they'd made of her hair tonight. He pushed her back against the rail, feasting on her lips and pressing himself against her, then groaned out his appreciation when she pushed right back.

Not to push him away, but to push herself closer.

And there was no question of pretending, then. There were no questions at all.

There was only this. Her. The two of them and the glory that swept through them, burning them both down where they stood.

Paris Apollo remembered, only vaguely, that they were standing outside. And that he had more to think about these days than his own pleasure. But that was the last thought he had as he wrenched his mouth from hers and stepped back to spear her with a dark glare that came from the very depths of him.

Because he was not certain that he could speak.

Her lips were parted, and, at last, he saw the way her chest moved, as if she were running a marathon. Better yet, there was that pink flush again, everywhere.

And Madelyn did not look as if she had the slightest inclination to stop running.

He did not ask himself why it mattered so much to him that she should be as transported in this moment as he was. That she should be as lost. As wrecked.

Paris Apollo bent and lifted her into his arms. Then, gazing down at her as if he'd never seen her before when he knew too well she was burned inside of him, he carried her into the palace. He shouldered his way into his rooms, striding with her to the bedroom that claimed pride of place far to the back and the bed that took over the better part of one wall.

He couldn't have said why it felt as if this was his true coronation. This moment as he carried the mother of his son to the bed where so many kings of Ilonia had lain in their time. He only knew that he had never felt like more of a king than he did as he laid her out before him on the grand mattress, then followed her down.

And he remembered everything.

The way he always had.

He remembered those Cambridge nights, the blazing fire between them, and the way she would sob in his arms. How time had lost its meaning, so deep inside her was he, as if they were one.

They had been one. He still believed that, no matter how it had ended.

She had made him insatiable, truly. He felt the same way again now, but more intensely, as if he'd been sober all these years and the taste of her tonight had swept him straight off the side of that wagon.

The only saving grace was that Madelyn looked as lost in this as he was.

He stripped that lovely dress off her body, not caring if it ripped. He shrugged out of his own clothes, kicking them aside.

Because every moment they were in each other's presence without being naked together, without skin touching skin, was a tragedy.

And there was too much time lost already.

Too many tragedies to name.

On the bed at last, he stretched out beside her and took a moment to look his fill. To revel in her before him like this once more.

"I can't bear this," she threw at him, though her voice was little more than a whisper. "I can't *bear this*, Paris Apollo."

She launched herself at him, the way she often had. For he had taught her what she knew, taking the innocence she'd given him, that tender gift. And she had never learned the jadedness that had marked so many of his encounters before her.

Nor had she learned it since, he found to his delight. She was eager, clumsy. Perfect.

And bright with this passion between them that made him feel as untutored and un-jaded as she was.

Madelyn crawled on top of him, and then her mouth was everywhere. Her hair fell down around him and he was lost in the warm scent that was only her, honey and a hint of salt. And in the slide of her lips across his cheekbone, his jaw.

He lay back as if he was sacrificing himself on an altar as she explored her way down the length of his body, making those low, greedy noises that had always driven him wild. He was torn between all the memories he'd held at bay that flooded him now and the glorious present, her mouth gliding where it liked and reducing him to little more than clay in her hands.

When she made it between his legs, where the truth of him stood tall and harder than steel, he sucked in a breath and ordered her away.

But she paid him no mind. Or perhaps he never quite got the command out because her mouth found him.

And in that sweet suction, that velvety heat, Paris Apollo let himself spiral all the way up to that edge, the flames dancing so high that he thought he'd turn to ash here and now—

Yet in the next moment, that beast in him roared— or maybe he roared out loud—and he was flipping her over, hauling her beneath him, and slamming his way into all of her wet, soft heat.

And then everything was golden.

Molten gold, impossible flame, and that maddening, glorious, drugging heat that was only and ever Madelyn.

Each thrust was better than the one before. Each gasp, each touch, a revelation.

There was the fury, the rage. There was the hurt, the need.

But beneath it was a deep kind of recognition.

A truth he was not sure he could name.

They tumbled this way and that. She rolled on top

and stayed there for a while, riding him with abandon. Then he could take it no longer and flipped her again, coming over her once more. He took her hands and hauled them up over her head so she arched against him, and both of them sighed out the sweetness of it.

All of it was sublime. None of it was enough.

Maybe he had known all along, back then and in all the years in between, that it never could be. That it never would be.

That there was only this woman for him.

No matter how he'd tried to pretend otherwise.

No matter how he'd failed to forget her.

Paris Apollo levered himself down, getting his face as close to hers as he could. And even though he could feel the way she trembled, right there on the edge, he slowed it down.

So slow that his whole body shook. So slow that he thought it might kill him, and her, too. And when she began to shake in earnest, he didn't stop. He maintained that same slick pace, throwing her over that edge.

Again and again, and then kept going.

Relentless. Inexorable.

Until she was sobbing out his name.

"We are each other's prison," he told her then, like an incantation. His voice dark like the night he moved through, meting out justice. Like the dark between them, slick and rich and studded bright with stars. "There is no key. There is only eternity, Madelyn. There is only this."

"Us," she whispered back, because she knew.

Because they both knew.

They always had.

And then, only then, did Paris Apollo let them both burn bright and finally fall, like comets far brighter than any lightning could ever be, through the dark night sky of their own making.

All the way back down to earth.

CHAPTER EIGHT

IT WAS DIFFERENT this time, Madelyn told herself.

Because she knew better. Because she'd been down this same road and knew it for the dead end it was, no matter what Paris Apollo might claim.

She had already survived him once. She would again. Of course she would.

That was the thing about being a mother. There was no room to brood herself into a state. There was no pacing around San Francisco this time, wishing the world might end so it would match how she felt inside.

She was going to have to live through this man again. No matter what happened.

And maybe because she had no expectations of happy endings this time, she was able to give herself over to the time they did have in a way she hadn't before. Because this time, she knew that these moments with Paris Apollo were precious and would be taken away again when this fever between them subsided.

No matter what he said.

"You act as if the very notion of being my queen is an insult," he said one night. He had insisted she join him and his ministers at a formal dinner, where everyone had peered at her as if she was a specimen beneath glass. Waiting, she assumed, for her to prove that she was an embarrassment to the crown.

She had taken a certain amount of pleasure in demonstrating the perfect manners that she had learned by watching some of the high-end guests at the resorts in Tahoe.

Paris Apollo had demonstrated his appreciation. Comprehensively.

"Not an insult," she murmured, her eyes closed as she lay pressed up against him, boneless with left-over delight. "But apprehensive, that's all. I already know how this will end."

"Do you, indeed."

She didn't heed the warning in his voice, the rumble she could feel beneath her ear. "Sooner or later, I will climb the wrong stair and find you barricaded behind another door. I accept it."

That was a lie. But in that moment, still burning up from the pleasure he gave her, it didn't feel like one.

Paris Apollo flipped her over, making her gasp a little, then laugh.

"I am a father now. A king," he told her, something fierce on his beautiful face. "And I do not betray the vows I have made, the promises I intend to keep."

Even though she knew better, Madelyn found she was tempted to believe him.

But then, wasn't that the trouble? She was always tempted where he was concerned.

And he took her again, in a passionate fury that had her sleeping so deep that she was sure she imagined waking—only slightly—to see him dressed in black again and leaving the room.

Particularly because he was there again in the morning, sleeping beside her when she woke with the sun.

"Your prison isn't so terrible, is it," he murmured another night, moving deep inside her. "You might live after all."

"Then again," she replied, her mouth against his neck, "I might not."

She would survive. Madelyn knew she would *survive*. But that wasn't necessarily *living*, was it?

Particularly because this time, she was less worried about the potential of other women circling Paris Apollo or locked bedchamber doors than she was about the times she woke up to find him gone. She found herself awake one night, her hand on the pillow beside her—gone cool—as she thought about that shadow she'd seen her first night here.

About the wall she knew he'd climbed then. About the reason a man might want tactical gear, especially the son of murdered parents.

And about the articles she read in the papers every

day that suggested someone was out there cleaning up the streets of Ilonia.

Madelyn didn't want to admit that she knew— that she *thought* she knew—who that someone was.

Yet in the daylight, it was difficult to brood too much about the fact that she was in a prison, no matter how beautiful and laced through with that particular Paris Apollo fire, when Troy found the whole experience so delightful.

Because he not only had a father, his father was a *king*.

"That makes me a *prince*," he told her with great authority. "And you're going to be a *queen*."

"Well." Madelyn had not expected the subject to come up over orange juice, but here they were. She cleared her throat. "You know, sweetheart, I don't have to become a queen for you to be the Prince here. You already are."

Troy looked at her as if she was very stupid but he loved her anyway. "I know, Mom. But you need to match."

That threw her more than she wanted to admit.

Later that morning, she actually succumbed to a dress fitting. And when it was finished, she let Paris Apollo's black-clad manservant regale her with tales of the previous King and Queen and their love for each other and adoration of the son they never thought they'd have.

"He came into this world a miracle," the man said. "But then, madam, all children should."

And that seemed to stick inside her ribs like a long, jagged knife.

She made her way outside into a bright summer's day. The palace seemed to be made of dreams and fairy tales, and the islands looked too good to be true. The moody Atlantic was blue today, the beaches white. The hydrangeas bloomed riotously everywhere she looked, dotting the hillsides, beaming alongside pathways, and flanking almost every doorway down into the parts of the main city that she could see from the palace grounds.

Today Ilonia didn't feel much like a prison at all. It felt like a dream come true.

Especially when she found her aunt sitting on a swing in the rose garden, watching Paris Apollo and Troy kick a soccer ball back and forth on the royal lawn.

Her heart squeezed so tight she had to stop walking and fight to breathe. Madelyn had to remind herself—sternly—of the six hard years she'd struggled through.

Almost entirely alone.

She found she had to do that a little too much as the days wore on.

"Maybe it's not all bad," said Corrine on one of their walks through the extensive palace gardens.

Back home in Tahoe, they had often tried to put in a bit of a summer garden in what summer there was so high up in the mountains. Unkillable geraniums seemed to be the height of their gardening prowess.

It felt a bit like a metaphor that even the gardens here were unutterably lush.

"There are worse things, of course," Madelyn allowed, trying not to sound disgruntled.

When, in fact, she felt disgruntled. She'd woken from strange, dark dreams to find Paris Apollo in the shower. He had bid her to join him and she had—but not after first noting that there was a pile of those black clothes in the bathroom hamper. *Almost* hidden. And then, in the shower, bruises on his knuckles. She couldn't understand why she hadn't asked him about those marks. Those clothes.

Why, instead, she had let him draw her to him and kiss her as if it had been another six years since they'd seen each other rather than a few hours.

She tried to focus on the present. On her marvelous aunt. On the fact that her son already thought it was settled that she was marrying Paris Apollo, and that, on some level, she must, too. Why else would she keep skipping her library hours for dress fittings and protocol consultations?

"It would be nice not to have any more financial concerns," she said now, grudgingly. Then smiled at Corrine. "And nicer still not to worry that I'm a burden on you."

"I remember when you came back from England," Corrine replied softly. "It was like he'd snapped you in two like a twig. But now he wants to marry you. That's a happy end to things, surely."

Madelyn told herself that there was something

wrong with her that her aunt's happy optimism, her saving grace these last years, only made her want to scream today.

"You'll have your last fittings today," Corrine was saying. "And I know you've set your heart against it, but you really do look like a queen in that dress, Madelyn. It's just stunning. *You* are."

And Madelyn could only smile and nod at her aunt, even as one hand lifted to her throat of its own accord and stayed there because she felt as if she were drowning.

The fact that Troy and Paris Apollo seemed to be having their own father and son love affair didn't help.

She should have loved that for Troy. She *did*.

But there was a gnarled and knotted, wholly reprehensible part of her that wished—only a little, and only when she was alone, and not in a way that she would ever admit out loud or act on in any way—that it could have been *slightly* harder for Paris Apollo.

That Troy could have been even *momentarily* wary of his father.

Just for a single, tiny, almost unnoticeable moment.

Every time that terrible thought surfaced, she hated herself for it.

But apparently not enough to keep it from resurfacing.

A few nights later, she was already feeling cranky and out of sorts when she made her way into the cocktail party she had only agreed to attend under duress.

I would not call this duress, Madelyn. Paris Apollo had laughed at her, kissing his way back up the length of her body. He had stood, smoothing his hands over yet another exquisite suit, which he had not wrinkled even slightly. She was the one who was limp. *More a religious experience, I think, given how often you called upon the Almighty, would you not agree?*

And really, it would have taken a far stronger woman than she had ever been in Paris Apollo's presence to argue.

She hadn't. Just as she hadn't argued when she'd come upon him unexpectedly in this hallway and watched his curiously green eyes light up—before he'd swept her into an alcove and showed her how easily he could make her come apart.

As if she wasn't already aware.

Madelyn had felt a bit inside out, to put it mildly. She'd made her way back to her rooms, taken a long bath, and spent a few hours with Troy and Corrine.

When her attendants came for her and told her it was time to dress, she didn't put up any resistance. Though she felt nothing but as she navigated her way through the palace, catching glimpses of her lush and glamorous dress in every mirror and gleaming surface she passed.

The usual deferential staff beckoned her along as she walked down the marble halls. Madelyn practiced her best friendly yet not-too-approachable smile as she nodded at each of them. She braced herself for the usual mix of Ilonian aristocrats and bureaucrats as she walked out into the raised courtyard that was already glowing with the lanterns strung from end to end.

And then, instead of practicing how to be graceful and regal, she stopped dead.

Because her parents were standing not far from the entrance, looking overwhelmed and ill at ease.

For a long moment, Madelyn could only stare at them. They stared back. She waited a long, agonizing moment, that same rash thought that had seized her up on that dais with Paris Apollo dancing through her again. Would they see that she had not let them down so badly after all? Would the fact that she was marrying an honest-to-God *king* make them proud of her at last? But another moment dragged by. Then another.

Only then did it dawn on her that they did not intend to rush to her or embrace her.

The way she did when she hadn't seen Troy for all of an hour.

She felt as if she was on some kind of roller coaster, racing through too many long-held emotions to name. And she realized that when she thought about her parents, she always thought about them as the daughter she'd been when they washed their hands of her. The daughter who had always longed to earn their approval.

The daughter who still hoped they might be proud of her again.

But while she would always be that daughter inside somewhere, that wasn't *all* she was any longer. She was also a mother now.

A mother who would never treat her son the way they had treated her.

Or were treating her right now.

She decided on the spot that she was proud of *herself*, thank you.

"Mom. Dad." Madelyn didn't know what else to say. She could see the palace staff moving in, warding off anyone who might try to venture near, and for once she was grateful for the damage control. The endless concern about *keeping up appearances*.

Her father cleared his throat. "We thought we would see the child," he said stiffly.

Madelyn blinked. She felt the searing heat of a deep, raw fury wash over her, but all she did was smile. "Did you come all the way here to see Troy? How funny. When you could have traveled far less distance and seen him in Tahoe at any time."

"Really, Madelyn," her mother said in that chastising tone of hers. "This is hardly the place."

Madelyn bit her tongue and did her best to glare at her parents without seeming to do so, because she knew there were eyes on her tonight. And would be forever, once the wedding happened.

She'd known full well that the wedding would mean she'd see her parents. The stern ministers had

been firm on that. *Optics*, they'd said. *Appearances.*
The truth of her relationship with them mattered far
less than how that relationship might be perceived
in the press.

*There will be those who feel the King married
below him,* one of them had told her, but in a brusque
sort of way that had made it impossible to tell if
he was one such person himself. *Analysis of other
royal relationships with commoners has led us to
conclude that the best defense is an offense that in-
cludes a united front, especially during the spectacle
of the wedding.*

Never fear, another had added. *Your role will no
doubt require as much separation from your former
life as you could wish.*

But Madelyn hadn't put together that said united
front would begin *tonight.*

*Why have you convinced yourself that you can
brush everything aside if it doesn't feel like this fairy
tale you want so badly?* she asked herself.

It was a rhetorical question. Because she knew
the answer to that already. She and Corrine had dis-
cussed her parents just the other day.

*I can't help but wish I hadn't disappointed them
so terribly,* Madelyn had said while Troy walked
with Paris Apollo down the length of the great gal-
lery, gazing up at so many paintings of boys who
looked just like him.

Corrine had made a little sound in the back of her
throat. *I never want to add fuel to a fire, Madelyn,*

but I will say that as far as I can tell, my sister was born disappointed. I know. I was there.

She thought of that now as the silence grew between her and her parents. And unlike so many of the times, growing up, that she'd fallen all over herself to fill these awkward spaces, this time she said nothing.

This time, she stood there as regally as possible. And waited.

"We received the news from an emissary of your…of the King," her father said after several moments inched by. He scowled at her. "He insisted that we come and support you."

"And, naturally, since a random king I doubt you've ever heard of insisted, you came at once."

"We heard of him when those rude journalists camped out on our doorstep," her father barked at her. "The neighbors will never look at us the same way."

"The horror," Madelyn murmured, with a bit more sarcasm than befitted an almost-queen.

"I see that the years haven't softened you any, Madelyn," her mother said with a sigh that made it clear she considered herself the victim here. "That's a shame."

Madelyn let out a laugh. "I didn't want to give Troy away. You wanted nothing to do with me unless I did. I'm not sure what *softening* would have done to make that scenario any better."

Her father made a low noise, as if registering how

concerning he found this conversation. But Madelyn kept her focus on her mother.

As ever, Angie Jones managed to look as if Madelyn was *doing* something to her. Possibly pummeling her where she stood. Or choking her. *Something* that she was *just* managing to fend off. Heroically.

The roller coaster inside her tossed her upside down, then flew through a few loops. Somehow, she kept from reacting to the sensation the way she wanted to.

"I worried all the way over here that this was just another way for you to sidestep the impact of your decisions," Angie said sorrowfully. She shook her head with pity. "I'm just so disappointed, Madelyn, that no matter what, you always look for the easy way out."

Madelyn didn't know what she might have said then. The roller coaster tossed her off into the air. She could feel her eyes opening wide and that same searing fury inside barreling through her to pool in the back of her throat, as if she was about to breathe fire.

But she didn't get the chance.

"Madam," came a lazy, amused voice she knew entirely too well, "I am a great many things. Most of them splendid indeed. But I can assure you, *easy* is not one of them."

Her mother made a strangled sort of sound. Her father began to look red around the ears.

Paris Apollo walked up beside Madelyn and slid his arm around her. She could feel the curious hardness of his palm, when, by any measure, he should have been soft. Pampered. It made her wonder exactly what he'd been up to in the Hermitage for two years.

She wondered about this a lot, but usually while she wasn't dressed.

"Ask anyone," Paris Apollo invited her parents. "I am remarkably hard work."

Madelyn could see that Angie and Timothy Jones—born and bred in Fresno, California—were wholly unprepared for King Paris Apollo of Ilonia.

She enjoyed that far more than she probably should have.

"If you'll excuse us," Paris Apollo said in his indolent way. "This is something of an engagement party for us. We're so pleased you could attend."

He whisked her away, seeming to see deep inside her with a single, searing glance, but she didn't forget her parents were there. Hunkering like dread in the corner of the evening and doing their best to suck all the light away. No matter how many people congratulated her. No matter how many times strangers complimented her and seemed to mean it. No matter how many people seemed to genuinely be excited that the King was marrying a regular woman.

"Like us," a woman said shyly when they were introduced. "But ever so much more beautiful."

Madelyn couldn't understand why her parents were the only two people at this party that she couldn't seem to impress.

Or why she still cared.

"You seem far away," Paris Apollo said as he ushered her out of the party some time later, leaving the guests to entertain themselves. Madelyn had been told this was the privilege of royalty. Tonight, she was glad of it.

"I'm right here," she replied.

Ungraciously, she could admit.

Paris Apollo stopped walking. They were in one of the grand halls of the palace, a stunning and airy architectural marvel of a room—but all she could see was the green of his eyes, the arch of his brow.

"You do not care much for your parents," he said.

And Madelyn thought that if she had to discuss them with him, here, she would shatter into pieces.

She would *break*.

"I don't want to think about them," she told him, knowing her voice was as urgent as the heat she could feel in her gaze. "I don't want to *think*, Paris Apollo."

His perfect mouth curved, slowly. So very slowly.

"I know just the thing," he promised her in a low voice.

And he was as good as his word.

It was raw, there in that bed of his that had begun to feel like some kind of chapel to her. It was a marvel in and of itself, what they could do to each other. The heights they could climb. The passion they could summon with a mere touch.

He wiped her clean. He made her new.

And when he rose, much later, and donned those dark clothes of his, Madelyn was not asleep.

Because her heart would not stop its terrible *beating* inside of her, leaving her aching and awake.

And because it was possible that she had forced herself to stay awake, knowing this would happen again.

That it wasn't a dream. That she wasn't seeing things.

That ignoring this was just another way of being the same foolish girl she'd always been, and if her parents' appearance here had made anything clear it was that she never, ever wanted to be that girl again.

Madelyn rose from the bed and dragged her gown back on, glad that it was one of the more comfortable ones. It even had pockets. She shoved her feet into her shoes, which were far less comfortable, but they would do.

And then she followed Paris Apollo out into the night.

CHAPTER NINE

PARIS APOLLO HAD been walking for some time when he realized he was being followed.

And was furious with himself because he should have noticed it sooner. He should have noticed someone behind him instantly, but he knew why he hadn't. He'd been too busy being lost in his head like some lovesick fool.

It was as if he was destined to forever be a letdown—to himself, to everyone around him—when it mattered most.

He had gotten well used to making his way out of the palace. And while he still sometimes climbed the wall to see if he could continue to evade his own guards efficiently, tonight he'd used a secret door set back in an overgrown part of the garden instead. It had been used by many a member of the royal family in times past. It had crossed Paris Apollo's mind that, really, he ought to have a word with the guards about how easy it was to enter and leave the palace undetected, but he hadn't. Because he liked the ability to come and go as he chose, the same as anyone.

On the other hand, no one had taken to his heels before.

And thanks to his inability to think of anything other than Madelyn, he had no way of telling if he'd picked up this tail before he left the palace or somewhere else along the way.

He'd taken the old path down the hillside, the one ancient Ilonians had carved with their own hands. The main part of the city was farther to the east, but he'd stayed to the west instead, crossing through one of the most exclusive neighborhoods on the island. It was all cobbled streets and graceful houses here, and his target was a particularly grand villa set out on a bluff by itself.

His cousin Konos's house.

Though he had to remind himself that Konos was not his quarry tonight. Paris Apollo still had a whole other level of Konos's henchmen to get through first. By now, Paris Apollo was certain that his cousin was well aware that someone—and, really, could it be any other someone?—was cutting a ruthless swath through his people.

All the people that Konos had used to enact his plan while he sat pretty and kept his hands clean. Making certain that any attempt to take him down by legal means—or even royal decree—would be risky at best. The courts would take too long. And after all the snide things Konos had said about Paris

Apollo, anything Paris Apollo did openly would be seen as retaliation.

Konos had the island's media in his back pocket. He would see to it personally.

These were the things Paris Apollo had spent his years in the Hermitage working out in his head like so many chess moves.

On this night, with only one full day left to get through before he married his queen and introduced his heir apparent to the kingdom as a *fait accompli*, Paris Apollo thought it might be entertaining to look in on his cousin. To see how things were going in his ever-shrinking world.

And to gloat a little bit. Maybe more than a little bit. Paris Apollo could admit that.

Because he knew that there had already been rumors about Troy's existence. Angelique Silvestri had talked to him about this quite seriously just the other day, as if she thought it was possible Paris Apollo wasn't aware of the whispers.

After tonight, with Madelyn and her parents discussing Troy so openly, he was sure the whispers would become shouts.

Konos and his pet newspapers would make sure of it, Paris Apollo had no doubt.

He was pleased with that. He was pleased with all of it, in truth. Everything was going to plan.

But clearly he was too pleased, because it hadn't occurred to him that someone might choose tonight to take advantage of his distraction.

He moved slower then, when what he wanted to do was run. The lanterns gleamed here, too, so he avoided the pools of light. And when he reached the end of the lane, he turned and walked toward the bluff. Hoping that whoever was following him would assume he'd rounded the corner and kept on toward the house on the bluff.

Instead, he used the shadows between the lanterns to secrete himself behind a tree, and waited.

It did not take long. The figure trailing him came around the corner in shadow, then stopped, looking this way and that before stepping into the light.

Paris Apollo felt everything in him freeze solid.

Because he was looking at Madelyn.

When that was impossible.

She hadn't even bothered to change out of the gown she'd worn to the party tonight. Her hair was as he'd rendered it personally, after several hours of tearing each other apart. It hung down to her shoulders and looked as if there had been hands in it.

There had been. His, and they ached to get back to it.

All this while she stood there, fully exposed. Anyone who happened by could see her, the future Queen of Ilonia, wandering around in the dark for no good reason.

He made as if to go to her, then stopped before he could. Maybe he shouldn't reveal himself. She clearly couldn't see where he'd got to. She was scowling, her hands finding her hips the way they often did when she was out of patience. Then she turned in circles, completely heedless of the fact that she was standing beneath the lantern and therefore in full view of anyone who might care to glance out a window.

She was not exactly stealthy.

The fact that he should stay hidden and make sure she failed to locate him was clear to him.

But it was no match for the kick of temper inside that took him over.

He stepped out from behind the tree and let the light catch him, too.

"What the hell do you think you're doing?" he asked in a low voice that carried on the night breeze.

Madelyn had been facing the other way just then, and she whipped back around, though she didn't look as startled as he would have liked.

As startled as she should have looked if she had a shred of sense.

"I think a better question is, what are you doing?" she shot right back at him. And then, apparently far more reckless than he'd ever given her credit for, she neither ran nor hid nor tried to dissemble. She simply lifted up her gown to keep it from dragging on the old road and marched straight for him.

Everything in him was that same riotous burn of temper, all of it focused on her. So intently that it made his blood seem to burn as it pounded through his veins. So deeply that he could feel the fire of it in his temples, his chest.

And his greedy sex.

Yet Madelyn continued to march toward him, uncaring or unaware, and stopped when she was a foolish handful of centimeters in front of him. If she was smart, she would have left a greater distance between them—for her own safety. He could feel that roaring beast within rouse itself, then focus in on her.

She was talking as if she had no idea of the danger she was in. "I saw you sneaking over the palace wall the first night I was here. Obviously, I assumed I was hallucinating. But no. You do this every night. *Every night*, without fail."

"You shouldn't be here, Madelyn."

"What can you possibly be thinking? You must know how dangerous it is to just be…out here. Roaming around."

"I am not at risk."

"You are the King, Paris Apollo. If it wasn't dangerous for you to be on your own, why do you have so many guards? So many walls around the palace? It only takes one motivated and disturbed individual to prove them all necessary. Just one. Are these nighttime rambles really worth that?"

"This does not concern you." It was a fight to keep his voice low. To keep from shouting—when Paris Apollo could not recall another moment in his life where he had come close to *shouting*. Somehow, he managed not to make this the first. "You should never have followed me away from the safety of the palace."

"Thank you for acknowledging that it's not as safe

as you're pretending," Madelyn said quietly, and it made that raw *intent* in him tip over into a kind of roar. "I can't understand why you'd risk yourself like this. What could possibly be so important?"

He wanted to rage at her, but it wasn't safe. Just because he couldn't see anyone peering out at them from any number of windows facing the street, that didn't mean there weren't eyes on them. Wasn't that what he been taught to assume, always, as a royal? That there were always eyes? It was only in places like the Hermitage that he could be sure he was truly on his own.

That was the true purpose of guards and walls. Above and beyond the relative few who liked to make threats that were usually idle, it was to ensure some small shred of privacy. Without them, he would have none.

But he did not feel that applied to this woman— *his* woman, soon to be his *wife*—and whatever had possessed her to come after him tonight of all nights. He hated her out here, alone. He hated that she was this close to his treacherous, murderous cousin.

He hated all of this.

Paris Apollo reached over and took her wrist in one hand, then began walking, tugging her with him as he went.

He expected her to fight. Because wasn't that what she did? Fight everything, at the slightest provocation? Fearless in the face of anything and everything—including him?

But tonight was strange in any number of ways. Because Madelyn did not try to wrench her wrist from his grasp. She fell into step with him, perhaps a bit too easily, as if they were simply a couple out for an evening stroll.

Though most people did not stroll about this far after midnight.

He skirted the bluff entirely, though there were lights blazing in his cousin's house. His jaw felt like granite as he thought of all the things he would not be learning tonight. All the gloating he would not get to do.

It was a wonder he didn't start shouting again, there and then. But he kept walking until he found the old, ancient gate at the end of a little-used side lane, tucked away between two elegant cottages that anyone else would likely think twice before approaching at this hour.

Paris Apollo was not anyone else. This was his island. And he knew every last centimeter of it like his own beating heart.

He led Madelyn to the gate that still opened the way it had when he was young, with a secret lever secreted in the midst of a flowering vine. Then he took her onto the steep path down to the beach beyond, where the tide was high and made it look as if there was nothing at the end of the path but a steep tumble into the water.

It was really no more than an optical illusion. And had the great benefit of keeping anyone who didn't know the beach's secrets away. For there was a turn in the trail that led back around beneath the hill to a private beach well out of the reach of the sea.

Once he'd navigated the way to the sand, liberally strewn with rocks and great pieces of driftwood, Paris Apollo dropped her hand. Like it was on fire. And then walked away because touching her was not doing anything good for his self-control.

"I will ask again," he said to the dark sky, to the covetous tide. To Madelyn herself, though everything in him was at a fever pitch already. "What possessed you to follow me? Tonight of all nights, when the island is filled with wedding guests. More suspicious eyes than usual."

"I could ask the same of you," she retorted. "I'm not sure there's ever a good time for the King to be wandering around in public, in the dark, all by his lonesome. But tonight of all nights? It's as if you *want* to be caught."

"I do not."

"And yet you didn't notice me behind you, when I doubt very much that I was giving the local cat burglars a run for their money." He had to grit his teeth at that, and he thought she knew. She tipped her head to one side, and he could see her too well in the dark. It meant she could see him, too. "Why won't you tell me what this is about?"

He didn't want to tell her. Or maybe it was the opposite. Maybe he had spent two years sitting with this and she was the only one he could think of to tell.

Every night, they came together and followed the fire that had always been between them, wherever it led. In the aftermath, they would lie together, with their breath coming fast and hard. And it would nearly burst out of him, the need to confide in her.

The way it always had.

"You can tell me," she said quietly, watching him far too closely. "Whatever it is."

And there was something in her voice then that made him pause. He barked out a laugh. "Do you think it's a woman?"

She didn't reply to that, which was a reply in itself, and he raked his hands over his face. He could not quite bring himself to laugh again. "You credit me with far more stamina than any man could have. Or do you not imagine that the demands we make on each other are more than enough for one person in one day?"

"I have *always* thought so," she replied, and he could see her eyes flash, there in the dark. Paris Apollo did not miss the emphasis on the word *always*.

"I was in my bedchamber when you returned that day," he told her, not sure why his voice had gone gruff. Only that there was something intense between them. There always had been.

"I know you were."

"Alone," he bit out. "With a very old bottle of very good scotch. I had instructed my staff to let no one in until I drank the whole of it down. I did not come out for two days." He scowled at her. "You were the one who left, Madelyn."

He watched his words fall through her, and he thought she swayed on her feet. Her lovely face, still too pretty, seemed to pale.

Yet she did not tumble over. She took a deep breath that sounded a great deal like some kind of grief, then stood taller.

Paris Apollo pushed on. "I'm not having an affair. I'm not sneaking out of my own palace for a little variety in my bed. And if I did, Madelyn, you can be certain that there would be no sneaking. I am a great many things, too many of them disgraceful, but I've never been a liar."

The waves crashed against the sand. Up on a nearby hill, a lighthouse beamed out over the water.

"I believe you," Madelyn said, surprising him. And he did not know, until she said it, how much he'd needed her to believe him. How much it mattered to him. It was another thing he hadn't seen coming, this need not only for her body, but for her to see who he really was. "But only because you've never been furtive a day in your life. Why now?"

It seemed to shake something loose inside him.

She believed him. She knew him well enough to know that what he said was true. He would not sneak around for sex. He never had.

There was not, as far as he knew, a single person alive or dead who had ever known him and believed that. They had all imagined that because his appetites were intense, he would do anything to feed them. Lie, cheat.

But even back in Cambridge, Madelyn had looked straight through to the heart of him. He had found it nearly painful then. Was it possible that some part of him had welcomed Annabel's take on Madelyn? Was it possible that he had believed in Madelyn's callousness a little too easily?

He had not known what to do with this intensity back then. It had overwhelmed him.

Tonight, he found it a kind of balm.

"It has never been much of a secret who ordered my parents killed," he told her then, simply enough, while the waves reached for them across the sand, again and again. "Not to anyone connected to the palace. My cousin Konos is an ambitious man. It has always been his intention to take the throne. He used to feed stories about my unsuitability to rule to the tabloids when I was all of thirteen. Fourteen. When there was supposed to be a media blackout until I reached eighteen. Instead, I was obliged to create a media persona much earlier. So that all my cousin's intimations would not be taken as fact. I did this by leaning into the things he said of me and making them seem charming."

She blew out a breath. And she no longer looked as furious as she had earlier, looking for him on a deserted street with her hands on her hips. Like she intended to give him—*him*—a piece of her mind whether he intended to marry her or not.

As if he was a man, not a king.

Paris Apollo began to feel that this was one more instance of all the ways she really would make the perfect Queen. It was entirely possible that she would understand what he was doing in a way no one else could.

For hadn't she come to find him in the Hermitage with a heart as hard as his had needed to be these past two years? Hadn't she kept his own child from him for five years?

If anyone knew the pleasures of revenge, he was certain it would be Madelyn.

"If everyone knows who killed your parents, why hasn't he been brought to justice?" she asked.

"Because he is the cousin of the King," Paris Apollo said with the same deep fury that accompanied even the thought of his cousin. "He is protected by his bloodline. And because there is no proof."

"This is what you've been doing," she said, frowning slightly. "Every night."

He wanted to reach over and rub that line between her eyes away, but he didn't. Touching her led to forgetting himself and his purpose. It was the only way he'd ever known how to deal with the intensity between them—but he was not the callow, overwhelmed princeling he had been at Cambridge. He had lived through a greater grief than losing her when once he would have thought that impossible.

Not that he intended to lose her again.

And now that he'd begun to tell her his story, he didn't want to stop.

It was as if he worried it would be trapped inside him forever. Though he knew it was a kind of madness to keep allowing himself to think these fanciful things that led him nowhere he needed to go.

Madelyn was still looking at him as if she was seeing him for the first time. "I've been reading the local papers and every day there's another story of criminals rounded up and dumped for the police to find. And just in case there's any confusion, they always have lists of their crimes pinned to the chest. This is you. *You* are doing these things. Your knuckles were bruised the other night."

"My parents should have lived for decades yet," Paris Apollo gritted out. "They should have had the opportunity to see their son act like a man and step into the role they crafted for him. But they didn't. They should have had the opportunity to know their grandson, but they won't. These things were taken from them. The man who arranged their deaths walks free, thinking himself safe as he plots to steal the throne from me, too, because that was the plan all along. Get rid of the old King and Queen, then make it clear that I am unfit. And I am certain that if that doesn't work as it should, some or other accident would be arranged for me, too."

"This is what the police are for. All you need to do is call and—"

"They were my parents, Madelyn. They thought

I was nothing short of a miracle, and their reward was that I shirked every responsibility they ever set before me." His voice was a kind of rasp, and he did not tell her that he had fallen in love with her long ago, and had loved her all the more because it would be the one thing his parents wanted for him that he could actually do. He shook his head to clear it of the past. "This is the very least I can do to honor their memories."

He genuinely expected her to nod, to agree. While he'd been talking, he'd moved closer without knowing he meant to move at all. He'd slid his hands to wrap tight over her slender shoulders, and if anyone had been looking at them then, they might have assumed this was a prelude to a passionate kiss.

Then again, everything was with Madelyn.

Paris Apollo saw her begin to shake her head.

He couldn't make sense of it.

"I've spent a long time beating myself up for the way I let my parents down," she told him softly. "I should have been the daughter they wanted, because I knew what their expectations were and I went ahead and let them down anyway. That's what I've been telling myself all these years. But then, tonight, they proved to me that it was never my fault. If I hadn't gotten pregnant with Troy, there would have been some other reason for them to wash their hands of me. Because that's actually what they want. No one in the world could possibly live up to their standards. They never wanted me to."

"My parents were nothing like that," Paris Apollo grated out. "If anything, they allowed me too much leeway in all things and excused it all away."

"I'm not suggesting otherwise." She moved closer, there in his arms, to press her fingertips on his chest. "They sound like truly wonderful people. I'm sorrier than you know that I never got the chance to meet them. That Troy never will. But that's not my point. I spent a lot of time these last years thinking about the many ways I could get revenge on my parents for turning their backs on me when I needed them the most. Sometimes it was all I thought about. And do you know what I finally understood tonight?"

"I do not want—"

"Revenge is a poison, Paris Apollo. It mires you in your worst moments while time marches on without you. It chains you to darkness. I know this. I lived this. And all the while I made up revenge scenarios in my head, my son—*our* son—was growing up. They tried to make me give him up. And I still spent far too much time in my head, which means I might as well have let them take him." She let out a soft breath. "Tonight made it all too clear. They don't have any power over me I don't give them."

"This is about justice, Madelyn. Revenge is just a happy byproduct."

"But…" She shook her head again and her gaze was imploring. And he didn't know what he was supposed to do when her gaze was the color of the sea just before dawn. When the world was so still and all manner of impossible things seemed attainable. "I haven't heard a single story about your mother and father that didn't make it clear that they were wise, generous, remarkable people. Every person I encounter, from the lowliest servant to ambassadors from afar, agree. They were all about love, Paris Apollo. That was who they were."

His chest hurt. "They were all that and more."

"Then you must know that they wouldn't want this for you," she whispered.

He felt as if her words inflicted a mortal wound upon him. He staggered back because he couldn't have his hands on her or hers on him. It felt like treachery and he was sick to death of treachery.

Coming from her, it felt like another betrayal.

He wished the moon wasn't rising tonight, dancing on the water as if nothing was the matter. He wished the stars did not dare to shine. He wished the waves themselves deserted this beach so that even they could not bear witness to one more instance of him being turned against.

One more bit of proof that the only people who had really believed in him were dead.

And given his behavior, he might as well have killed them with his own hand.

"And, pray tell, what do you know about love?" He hardly recognized his own voice then. It was so harsh. As if every syllable was made of acid, but he struck out anyway. Wasn't that who he'd made himself? "Where would you have learned it? Certainly not from your parents. Certainly not from a brief, ill-considered affair with a man you washed your hands of before you left the country."

"I did no such thing." But she sounded winded. And he felt hollow. "I knew you were faking. *I knew it.*"

"I *wanted* to forget," he growled. "I wanted you to think I thought *that little* of our time together. Is that what you would call love? That pettiness? Tell me, Madelyn—is that where you got all this wisdom you dispense so freely?"

For a moment she looked unsteady, but then, while he watched, she straightened. She stood taller, even shifting her feet farther apart as if to take up more ground. She folded her arms and eyed him steadily.

It only made his ribs ache all the more.

"I know all about love," she said in that mild yet brutal way that he decided, there and then, enraged him. "I think I must have fallen in love with you at first sight. That was why it was so all-encompassing. That was why, on some level, I think we were both relieved it had to end when I flew home. And then it was easier to pretend that it had been something shabby and coarse, didn't it? But it was neither of those things. It was love, Paris Apollo. I was there. I know."

He opened his mouth to tell her the lie that would end this, once and for all. But he couldn't do it.

And it was as if she knew. She took a step closer, and he didn't like that. He liked it less when she took another. "You are the only one I have ever loved, in all my life. The only one I will ever love. And I know it's the same for you, whether you want to admit it or not."

That was another attack, a strike straight to the core of him. "I am incapable. Ask anyone."

And maybe he was finally shouting, after all.

But it must have been inside him, because she was still speaking in that quietly devastating way. "I don't need to ask a soul. *I know.* It was the same for both of us. It's still the same for both of us. And we spent the past six years differently, but it all amounts to the same thing. Love, Paris Apollo. And I don't think it matters when or how we found each other again. It would always be like this. It will always be like this."

"You had no intention of ever informing me of my own son's existence. I somehow doubt that has the makings of a love for all ages, Madelyn. You're starting to sound like a silly little virgin all over again."

"I think we both know that I'm no such thing. You saw to it personally." He wasn't prepared for that, or for the way her mouth curved as if she found this…amusing.

Or anything less than absolutely devastating.

"It isn't loving each other that hurts us, Paris Apollo," she told him then, in that same quiet voice that pounded inside of him, drowning out the sea all around him and even his own heartbeat. "It's the pretending that we don't. It's the pretending that we're something less than what we are. That we weren't stuck by lightning that very first moment, and staggered around, half burned and half electric, trying to make sense of it when there was no sense to be made. Sometimes that's the way it is. Two people meet and they're meant for each other, and sense has nothing to do with it.

"Madelyn, for God's sake—"

"And even if I didn't already know this to be true about you and me, I know it because of Troy," she continued, with that soft precision that he feared might well be the end of him. "He's the perfect embodiment of the love between us and you know this. I know you do. I watch you with him. I see the way you look at him, then at me, as if you can't believe we made him. But we did."

He wanted to end this. He wanted to walk away, but he couldn't seem to move.

"And do you know how we made him, Paris Apollo? With love. There is not a single cell in his body that didn't come from love. He's the proof, if you need it. The walking, talking, thrilled-he-gets-to-be-a-prince *proof*."

Paris Apollo didn't want to talk about Troy. He didn't want to bring that bright, funny little boy into this, because he was separate. He was something else.

Or, possibly, he had something to do with that yawning chasm deep inside Paris Apollo that he had no intention of looking at too closely. He tried to shove it all away.

"You can talk about love all you wish," he managed to get out. "I can't stop you. But that has nothing to do with the course I am bound to take here."

This time, she was the one who closed the distance and put her hands on him. She gripped his arms, still looking up at him, her expression as much beseeching as it was infuriated.

That, too, made him ache.

"There are courts for a reason," she said, her voice urgent. "You need to be a king, not a vigilante. You need to be a father, Paris Apollo. A husband. A man." She gripped him harder. "And I know that you can be a good one. I know that you *are* a good one.

But that was the final straw because Paris Apollo knew better.

Within him, he was nothing but bitter storms and despair, guilt and rage.

He stepped back. He made certain to look at her as coldly and as cuttingly as he could.

Because he couldn't have this. He couldn't be the man he sometimes saw when she looked at him. He couldn't be anything but what he was—a creature better suited to the darkness, made only for revenge and restitution.

The man who had loved her and lost her once, and then lost everyone else he'd loved. Suggesting the common denominator was him.

If he was even a shadow of the man his parents had imagined he might be, he would never risk Madelyn like this. Much less an innocent child.

He gathered that shadow around him now.

"You are entirely mistaken about me," he said, the cold of a thousand winters in his voice. "Must I prove that? Very well."

Madelyn whispered his name. It rang like a bell, deep inside him. Like all the churches whose doors he dared not darken.

"I release you," he told her harshly. Because it was better that way. "I will instruct the palace that the wedding is called off. You and Troy can go home to your lake and your woods, with my compliments."

Then he turned and left her there, standing on a hidden beach. He didn't look back.

Not until he was far enough up the path that when he did look, the beach had disappeared in the curve of the hill and there was nothing but the sea and the moon far above.

As if she'd never been there at all.

CHAPTER TEN

MADELYN STOOD ON that beach for a long time.

And when, at last, she turned and started back up the path, she hardly knew how she managed to put one foot in front of the other.

She didn't understand how she was here again. How had she given this same man her heart *again* only to have him smash it once more?

She wandered without paying any attention to where she was going until it occurred to her that everything she'd said to Paris Apollo was true for her, too.

Ilonia seemed at times a fairy-tale kind of place, but it was all too real. Paris Apollo's parents had been murdered, for God's sake. It was just as dangerous for a future queen—or an ex-future queen, to be precise—to wander like this as it was for a king.

Or anyway, it was putting an unnecessary target on her back.

Madelyn found it helpful to have something to concentrate on. To figure out where she was, which was easy enough in a place she hardly knew because all she needed to do was look up to see the palace standing there at the top of the hill. She let it lead her home.

But when she got to the palace, sneaking back in that same gate, she didn't slink off to her own rooms the way perhaps she should have. Instead, she smiled serenely at the guards and assorted night staff she passed in the halls as she made her way to Paris Apollo's rooms instead.

She could admit to herself that she'd expected him to be there, perhaps brooding out on his terrace. But he was nowhere to be found in the vast, sprawling apartments. She searched each and every room, but they were all empty.

Madelyn decided that she would wait for him.

She crawled onto his bed, where she had sobbed out his name in pure joy more times than she could count in these last weeks, curled herself into a ball, and expected that she would stay wide awake.

Instead, she slept. And hard.

When she woke, it was to find light streaming into the room, indicating that the sun was high.

But Paris Apollo was still nowhere to be seen. There was no indentation on the side of the bed where he normally slept. She had the sinking feeling he hadn't come back here at all.

She felt woozy and tired. And her heart ached as if it hadn't been ripped right out of her chest on that dark beach.

Madelyn wanted to lie down. And stay there. But instead, she pushed herself up and onto her feet. And even though she wanted nothing more than to go directly down into the main part of the palace to start questioning the staff as to Paris Apollo's whereabouts, she knew that there were too many wedding guests here.

Including her own judgmental parents, who she knew a little better today than she really wanted to. The last thing she needed to do was give them ammunition by appearing in last night's dress, looking bedraggled.

So she took the longer, more private route back to her own rooms and was happy to find her trio of attendants within.

"I need to find the King," she told them briskly.

"He's not here, madam," one of them said, sounding cheerful despite the quizzical look on her face.

"And we are to pack," said another. "Straight away."

The third looked alarmed. "Begging your pardon, of course."

That Madelyn did not scream bloody murder was, she thought then, a mark of her character.

Instead of screaming the way she wanted to, she left the three of them to their packing and headed deeper into her rooms. She took a shower and fixed her own hair for a change, like the grown woman she was. She checked in on Troy and Corrine, con-

firming that while Corrine had heard the news, no
one had broken it to Troy.

"Let's make sure no one does," Madelyn suggested under her breath.

"That's the spirit," Corrine replied, with her usual
optimistic grin.

As ever, it was exactly what Madelyn needed.

She kissed Troy even when he tried to wiggle
away in mock-horror that would likely be real in
ten years—so she would kiss him all the same—
and then set off. She took advantage of the exquisite
clothes that had been provided for her. They accorded
her an authority she knew perfectly well she didn't
convey when dressed in her preferred jeans. Even
with her hair piled up on the top of her head like a
commoner and last night's hard sleep on her face, she
knew that what the staff would see was their queen.

No matter what Paris Apollo might have ordered.

That was how she wound her way into the mu-
nicipal part of the palace and found herself knocking
on the door of Angelique Silvestri's office, without
anyone daring to block her way.

"I heard a terrible rumor," the older woman said
when Madelyn walked in.

"I heard the same one myself when I woke up,"
Madelyn agreed. "From all sides."

The minister gazed back at her. "Is it true?"

"I don't know how it was phrased. Or how this
news was delivered to you. But I was not consulted."
She held the older woman's gaze. "I do not agree."

And then held her breath because there was no telling how the other woman would respond.

It took a moment. Another. Then Angelique's poker face cracked, just enough to allow the faintest curve of her lips. "Splendid."

"No one seems to know where he is," Madelyn said then, though she felt significantly lighter, suddenly.

"He's gone back to the Hermitage," Angelique replied. In a mild tone that only got milder as she went on. "He is not to be disturbed by anyone. And, most specifically, you are not to follow him."

Madelyn took that in. It shouldn't hurt, because she had already been hurt enough... But it turned out there was always more hurt to be had. She straightened her shoulders. "I would prefer not to follow those instructions."

Angelique stood from her desk, looking smooth and unwrinkled. "I quite agree." She paused then. For a long moment. "I am the King's godmother, as perhaps you know."

"I didn't know." Madelyn studied her. "But that makes sense. I don't think anyone else would have kept tabs on Troy and me for so long without interfering otherwise."

"Queen Neme was my dearest friend," Angelique said quietly, for once sounding nothing at all like the dragon lady who had appeared on Corrine's doorstep and changed all their lives. "It was a surprise to everyone when she caught King Aether's eye. To everyone but me, that is. It is not an exaggeration to say that she made everyone around her better, simply because of who she was. She was that joyful. She was that *good*. Every day, I wish she was still here."

"I wish I could have met her. I wish my son could have."

Angelique looked away, and Madelyn followed her gaze to the framed photograph that stood alone on her mantel. It was of two girls, one laughing as if she was made of sunshine. And the other gazing into the camera, looking far more serious, with hints of the fearsome minister she would become one day already there in her youthful face.

"Neme and the King loved each other very much," Angelique continued, her voice softer. "But when years had passed and she had suffered more losses than anyone should have to bear, she decided that she would leave the King."

Madelyn, who should have been itching to get away herself, to go find Paris Apollo, instead found that she was deeply invested in this story. Her hand crept over the place where her heart should have been. "Why?"

"Because he was the King of Ilonia. He needed an heir." Angelique sighed. "She loved him so much that she was willing to give him up so that he could fulfill his duty to his country."

But Madelyn knew the Queen hadn't left the King. And that a version of this story was how the palace was selling the years she and Paris Apollo had been apart, so she smiled. "And I take it he loved her enough to tell her that there was no point in his duties, or anything else, unless she was with him."

Angelique's eyes gleamed then. She nodded, slowly, and in those two small gestures, Madelyn could see the old King and Queen in a new way. As more, somehow, than the stories so many people had told her about them. As people in their own right. Who had loved here and lost too much but chose love again.

As if she could read Madelyn's mind, Angelique crossed the room, then stopped beside her.

"Love is always the answer," the older woman said. "And you can take it from me that no matter what my godson might have said to you to break off this wedding, I tracked him. His parents did not wish to know the details of his wild days, but I did. And I know who he loved, Madelyn." She reached over and took Madelyn's hand, squeezing it once, hard. "Who he loves."

Madelyn felt that stinging at the back of her eyes again. There was a lump in her throat. "Good," she replied. "Because so do I."

And this time, she and Angelique Silvestri smiled together, finally in perfect accord.

Madelyn didn't need to be urged out of the SUV when it drove her off the ferry that Angelique had commandeered, then brought her to that little parking area halfway up the lonely mountain. She thanked the driver, then charged up the narrow path cut into the side of the mountain as if she had something to prove.

Because she did.

And it was probably wiser to get as much of her jagged, furious energy out before she reached the Hermitage.

Only because she didn't think that it would serve anyone if she went in there after him, guns blazing.

She already knew where that would lead. And she needed this to be different. She had to find some way to make this *different* from what had come before.

Once she got to the Hermitage's gates, she worried that it was entirely possible Paris Apollo might have locked her out. If he'd had the slightest suspicion that she would come up here after him.

But when she reached the door, a simple push opened it up, and she found herself in that stone court once more.

This time, he did not come out to greet her.

Madelyn made her way inside, finding nothing but stone and memories of her first night here. When she had been so overwhelmed by Paris Apollo and unable to believe she was actually seeing him again. In the flesh.

It made her feel a bit flushed and unsteady on her feet to think of how far she'd come from that night here. And how far there was still to go.

She blew out a breath and didn't head up to the upper levels, where she already knew there were bedrooms everywhere and more lounges like the one she and Paris Apollo had stood in that first night, with narrow windows and a storm outside. This time, she headed to the lower levels instead.

Because this time, the storm was already inside.

In her mind's eye, she could see the pictures she'd looked at of this place. She'd seen the various levels stacked on top of each other, so she knew that she wasn't really descending into any kind of cave.

But it felt like one.

Down at the bottom of the spiral stairs that wound around the interior of a stone tower, she found herself standing before a huge door made of metal hinges and sturdy oak. It looked ancient. It looked forbidding.

Madelyn tugged on the heavy iron handle and let herself in.

Before she could talk herself out of it.

But then she had to stop in astonishment when she saw what waited for her.

The door opened up to a great room. Like a kind of loft, except it was carved into the stone and the rough edges made it clear it really was a kind of cave after all. As if whoever had made this level hadn't bothered to finish the part of the room's walls that were just…mountain.

Yet every other part of the space was modern.

This, she realized, was Paris Apollo's command center. This was how a king could disappear from his people for two years yet still run his country.

There was a wall entirely made up of screens.

There was what she assumed was a state-of-the-art computer console. There was an area set aside for what looked like a private gym, equipped with fierce-looking machines and iron things that looked like yokes, plus barbells and more weights than could possibly be necessary for one man. Behind it, she could see that a climbing wall had been fashioned out of the slope of the mountainside that formed the ceiling.

And the side of the room that faced the islands outside was all glass. A simple glance told her that her initial impression, back on that stormy night when she'd first come here, had been right.

She could see the palace, away in the distance two islands over, standing high and proud. She could see the other islands that made up the rest of Ilonia, scattered across the sea like gleaming green marbles.

But most important, she saw Paris Apollo standing in the center of this place of his, glaring back at her.

He was stripped to the waist. And even now, even after everything that happened and everything that had been said on that beach, she felt that same longing for him that she always did. She could see all of those ridged muscles she had explored with such dedication, and below them, that dusting of dark hair that led to his sex.

He was still the most beautiful man she'd ever seen. He was, and would always be, the great love of her life.

And he was looking at her now as if she'd been sent to assassinate him herself.

She watched as he braced himself. He squared his shoulders as if he fully anticipated that she would come in swinging.

And Madelyn had intended to. She had thought of nothing but the many things she would hurl his way as she stormed up the side of this mountain.

But as she stood here and really looked at him, so terribly alone and so dedicated to his guilt and the things he felt he needed to prove to the ghosts of the two people who had always forgiven him for everything, she felt, instead, the heart she'd thought he'd stolen from her beat hard and painful in her chest. She felt her eyes fill up with tears.

Madelyn moved toward him and didn't care the way she probably should have when those tears swelled up and spilled over, making hot trails down her cheeks. She walked to him, as carefully if he was some kind of wild animal, but she wasn't afraid.

Even when he looked at her as if he might come apart at any moment, she still wasn't worried.

She walked directly to him. She reached up and fit her palms to his face, one on each side of his strong, perfect jaw.

"Madelyn," he growled out in warning.

But she could hear that longing beneath it.

So she *shushed* the King of Ilonia. She held him.

And she whispered, "Paris Apollo, they would

never ask this sacrifice of you. You are a father your-self now. You know better."

He made a noise and looked as if he wanted to pull away, but she held on.

She held his gaze, though hers was blurry. "Think," she urged him. "Is this how you want your own son to mourn you one day? Is this the lesson you want him to learn?"

CHAPTER ELEVEN

ALL THE FIGHT within Paris Apollo bled out of him then.

All the fury that had propelled him here today disappeared as if it had never been.

Because she was right. His parents would never have wanted this, not any of this. They would have delighted in Troy. They would have played with him and laughed with him, and they would have found his mother a marvel just as Paris Apollo did.

They had wanted nothing for him but happiness.

He put his hands on top of hers, holding them there. Trapping them. "I don't know how to do this," he grated out.

And Madelyn, his beautiful Madelyn, with her face wet with tears and the world he didn't deserve in her eyes, gazed back at him as if he really was the man she had described on that beach last night. "I don't think anyone does. Not really. It's all a lot of muddling and hoping for the best. All the best things in life are that way, I'm pretty sure."

"All I do is let them down," he said, his voice

low and gruff. "My parents. My people. You. Troy. It is inevitable."

"Everybody lets the people they love down now and again," Madelyn whispered back fiercely. "It's called being a complicated person. It's part of being alive. What matters is what you do next. Not how you broke it, but how you choose to fix it. How you *try*."

Paris Apollo stood there, in this room where he had trained and planned, raged and mourned. And even though the light of this summer's day poured in, as ever, he had only seen the darkness.

Until Madelyn walked in and brought the sun with her.

And suddenly, he couldn't bear that they were separated. By these two inches, by the clothes they wore.

But not, for once, in that too-wild, too-untamed way that everything had been between them since she'd come to Ilonia. Since they'd met, for that matter.

Today he thought about all the things she'd said to him on that dark beach. He thought about loving her, not losing her.

And this time he kissed her, not with desperation, but with hope.

Slow, sweet, devastating hope.

He took his time. He helped her out of her clothes, then kicked off his trousers.

He lost himself in the way she smiled at him,

bright with that joy he'd always craved, and then even wider when he smiled back.

They had taken each other too many times to count. He had tasted her so often and so well it should have been impossible to find anything new, but he did.

As if she was brand new to him every time.

The woman he loved. The woman he had always loved.

The only woman for him, just as she'd said.

He pulled her down with him onto the softest of the rugs that were thrown only sparingly across the floor here. And he made his lazy way down her body, easing her over onto her belly so he could spend some quality time with the nape of her neck, the enchanting indentation along her spine, the flare of her hips and pert bottom. He found his way to the mysteries beneath, curving his fingers around to find the center of her need, slick and hot.

And slowly, but not so sweetly, he set her alight.

When he turned her over again, he looked down at the way she was splayed out before him. The way she gave herself to him in all this light pouring through the glass.

And Paris Apollo understood that whatever came after, these were their vows. This was their ceremony.

He could see on her face that she knew it, too.

"I love you," he told her, though he had never said those words out loud to anyone save his parents. And though her eyes got bright with emotion, he didn't stop. "I was so in love with you in Cambridge that it made me a stranger to myself. I had to get appallingly drunk to keep myself from chasing you home. If I'd known you came back, I knew I would never have let you leave."

"I love you, too," she told him, solemn and certain. "I have always loved you, too."

He fit his hands over her sweet belly that had nurtured his son. "I'm so sorry that I missed this," he whispered. "That I missed every change in this beautiful body of yours. That I wasn't there to worship you as you deserve and keep you from struggling and worrying for even a moment."

She whispered his name, though it was a broken sound, but he didn't mistake it for anything but the joy that danced all around them now, like a moon across the water in the bright light of the summer day.

"It is easier to plot revenge than it is to do this," he confessed to her, gazing up at her. "My parents loved each other so completely, so fully, that no one who came near them was ever in any doubt. I have never known how they did it. I never thought that I was capable of such emotion, but then I looked up in a pub and there you were."

"I remember." Her smile widened. "And I can't believe you pretended you didn't."

"Maybe I wanted to believe I *could* forget you," he said, drinking her in. "Because otherwise, what would be required of me? That I...*feel* all of that again? That I feel it forever?"

"Yes," Madelyn whispered, still smiling, as if she'd known all along. "It requires everything."

Paris Apollo trailed kisses from her navel to one breast, then the other, anointing them both with his tongue. "I will make myself vulnerable. I will open myself to you, Madelyn, and show you all these dark things in me. For you, and my son, I will give whatever you wish. Whatever is needed. Whatever makes us whole."

"And I will do the same," she said, wiping at her face, though her smile was so wide he thought he could lose himself in it. "I promise you, I will not make up stories in my head and decide they're real. Never again. I promise you that I will not treat our child the way my parents treated me, never good enough. Always on pins and needles, waiting for the other shoe to drop. I want him happy. So loved it never occurs to him to doubt it."

"How could he be anything else?" Paris Apollo asked.

She moved against him, making him suck in a breath. "And I'd like him to be the first, Paris Apollo. Of many."

A family, Paris Apollo thought, letting the notion take hold of him. He had lost a family, and now he'd gained one. He only wished he could tell his parents that their fondest dreams for him had finally come true.

"I don't know how I am so lucky," Paris Apollo told her then. "But I promise you, Madelyn, I will do all I can to make you feel this lucky in return. Every day, for the rest of your life."

And then, there on the floor where he had wrapped himself in darkness for years, Paris Apollo and the woman who loved him even when he was not sure he loved himself found their way to light.

Again and again and again.

Later, he made a brief phone call to the staff back at the palace, telling them that the wedding was still on.

And because he was their king, they acted as if they had never doubted that it would be so.

Or perhaps that was down to his queen.

Then he and Madelyn renewed the vows they had just made in every possible way they could. They ate, sitting on the counters in the kitchen and telling each other stories. They sat in the sauna and then stood out in the cold, laughing at the rush of sensation it brought. They made love, at last, and over and over again.

In the morning, they went down to the palace once more. Truly united.

And that was where they became the King and the Queen of Ilonia, presented the Crown Prince to the kingdom, and proceeded to live happily and joyfully forever.

Because Madelyn would have it no other way.

And Paris Apollo was besotted—openly—and

made sure that whatever she desired, whatever she needed, she got.

By royal decree, if necessary.

CHAPTER TWELVE

TROY MET HIS grandparents at the wedding and was not impressed.

"You don't live in California," he said distinctly. Angie and Timothy frowned at him, making Paris Apollo consider calling for the guards. "If you did, you would visit us."

"Out of the mouths of babes," Paris Apollo murmured, and only smiled when his bride shot him a quelling look.

"Thank you for coming," said the new Queen of Ilonia to the two dour-faced people who did not deserve to call themselves her parents. "It meant more than you know."

And when she turned back to the reception that spilled out onto the palace's sloping lawn, she held Troy's hand on one side and Paris Apollo's on the other.

Her real family, Paris Apollo thought. And his.

He listened to his new wife and stopped hunting down criminals in the night. He met with the police instead, telling them what he knew and, better yet, what he suspected.

Justice was slow, but Madelyn was right. It was better that way. And five years later, Paris Apollo stood in the High Court and watched as his cousin was finally sentenced for his role in the murders of King Aether and Queen Neme.

He expected to feel let down. To think it was too little, too late, or that it no longer mattered, but he didn't.

It felt good. Right.

And he felt ready to move on with his life now that Konos was getting what he deserved.

Because Paris Apollo certainly had better things to think about than his cousin's unhinged plots or his own revenge. Like his beautiful wife, his marvelous queen, whose first order of business while taking it easy in the palace had been to finish her degree. Because, she told him with a laugh, she really didn't like leaving things undone.

She took what courses remained at the University here in the islands, making it impossible for his people to do anything but adore her.

And when she was done, she opened a home for single mothers on every island in Ilonia and an international charity to work on doing the same all over the world. She called it Corrine's House because— she said at the gala event to open her new endeavor, with her proud husband and beloved aunt standing at her side—everyone deserved to be lucky enough to live in Corrine's house when they needed it most.

Just as she had.

Another preoccupation of Paris Apollo's was showing his people who he really was. Not the indolent wastrel. Not the vigilante only some had seen or even suspected. But the man that Madelyn knew he could be.

The man who tried to be good so that he could be a decent king.

And over time, when his people cheered for him, Paris Apollo knew that they meant it. They weren't giving him a pass. They weren't hoping he would grow up.

He worked hard to make sure he was the King they deserved.

And when he and Madelyn were not trying their best to live up to their own best expectations of who they could be and what they could achieve, they were focused on their favorite part of their life together.

Their family.

"You'll have to help me," Paris Apollo told Troy when they found, to their joy, that Madelyn was pregnant not long after they were married. "You've been the man of the house for so long. I have to make sure I live up to your example."

"It's a lot of work," Troy replied very seriously. "But I think you can do it."

Paris Apollo dedicated himself to the task. He felt the time he'd missed in Troy's life keenly, so he tried to make up for it. He had his own parents' example, always, and so he knew it fell to him to make sure that his duties never got in the way of being a good father. And that being a good father meant allowing Troy to be who he was, not who Paris Apollo wished him to be.

And as for the brothers and sisters who followed Troy, all named for glorious cities in antiquity—because they liked a theme—Paris Apollo never took for granted the time he got to croon songs to them while they were still in their mother's belly. Or to make sure that Madelyn knew that she only became more beautiful to him when she was big and happy with his child. Or sometimes not so happy, which allowed him to dote on her the way she would never permit him to do otherwise.

Troy's first younger sister was born into Paris Apollo's hands. He held her after the doctors wrapped her up, then lay her in Madelyn's arms.

"I almost missed this," he whispered as the tiny, perfect girl slept in her mother's arms.

"I climbed that mountain to get you," Madelyn reminded him. "Twice. I was going to make sure you didn't miss a thing."

And when she told him she wanted to make Angelique Silvestri their new daughter's godmother, Paris Apollo felt the circle come complete within him.

Maybe he couldn't have his parents, but he had

this world that they'd made better and all the people who still loved them.

And those were gifts he did not intend to squander.

As the years passed, and the palace was alive again with a king and a queen and their big, rowdy brood to go with it, Paris Apollo often found himself down on that bench at the farthest edge of the palace gardens.

It was another secret spot that was impossible to see from a distance but where, if he sat and waited, it was almost as if he could see his parents out there amongst stars. Dancing in the moonlight over the waves of the sea the way he'd watched them dance when he was a child.

That was where he sat some nights, after the children were in bed, and talked to his parents the way he wished he had when they were alive. That was where Madelyn would come and join him, sitting beside him so he could wrap her up beneath his arm and breathe in the life they'd made here. The family they'd created.

The love they tended, every day, trimming back the things that didn't bloom and cherishing the things it did.

And some nights, they would look at each other and one or the other would lift a challenging brow.

Then off they would go to find that secret doorway that allowed them to sneak out into the streets of the island together—but always with a guard who stayed a respectful distance behind them.

Because this wasn't about recklessness. This wasn't about revenge.

But to celebrate love, and each other, and these islands he had always loved and Madelyn had come to love with him.

And they would walk, hand in hand, from one lantern to the next, shining brightly in the night.

The way they did everything that mattered.

Together.

* * * * *

Were you captivated by
A Secret Heir to Secure His Throne?
Then make sure you check out these other stories by Caitlin Crews!

Crowning His Lost Princess
Reclaiming His Ruined Princess
Willed to Wed Him
The Christmas He Claimed the Secretary
The Accidental Accardi Heir

Available now!

#4097 A BABY TO MAKE HER HIS BRIDE
Four Weddings and a Baby
by Dani Collins
One night is all Jasper can offer Vienna. The people closest to him always get hurt. But when Jasper learns Vienna is carrying his baby, he must take things one step further to protect them both... with his diamond ring!

#4098 EXPECTING HER ENEMY'S HEIR
A Billion-Dollar Revenge
by Pippa Roscoe
Alessandro stole Amelia's birthright—and she intends to prove it! Even if that means working undercover at the Italian billionaire's company... But their off-limits attraction brings her revenge plan crashing down when she discovers that she's carrying Alessandro's baby!

#4099 THE ITALIAN'S INNOCENT CINDERELLA
by Cathy Williams
When shy Maude needs a last-minute plus-one, she strikes a deal with the one man she trusts—her boss! But claiming to date ultrarich Mateo drags Maude's name into the headlines... And now she must make convenient vows with the Italian!

#4100 VIRGIN'S NIGHT WITH THE GREEK
Heirs to a Greek Empire
by Lucy King
Artist Willow's latest high-society portrait is set to make her career. Until the subject's son, Leonidas, demands it never see the light of day! He's everything she isn't. Yet their negotiations can't halt her red-hot reaction to the Greek...

#4101 BOUND BY A SICILIAN SECRET
by Lela May Wight

Flora strayed from her carefully scripted life and lost herself in the kisses of a Sicilian stranger. Overwhelmed, she fled his bed and returned to her risk-free existence. Now Raffaele has found her, and together they discover the unimaginable—she's pregnant!

#4102 STOLEN FOR HIS DESERT THRONE
by Heidi Rice

After finding raw passion with innocent—and headstrong—Princess Kaliah, desert Prince Kamal feels honor-bound to offer marriage. But that's the last thing independent Liah wants! His solution? Stealing her away to his oasis to make her see reason!

#4103 THE HOUSEKEEPER AND THE BROODING BILLIONAIRE
by Annie West

Since his tragic loss, Alessio runs his empire from his secluded Italian *castello*. Until his new housekeeper, Charlotte, opens his eyes to the world he's been missing. But can he maintain his impenetrable emotional walls once their powerful chemistry is unleashed?

#4104 HIRED FOR HIS ROYAL REVENGE
Secrets of the Kalyva Crown
by Lorraine Hall

Al is hired to help Greek billionaire Lysias avenge his parents' murders...by posing as a long-lost royal *and* his fiancée! But when an unruly spark flares between them, she can't shake the feeling that she *belongs* by his side...

HARLEQUIN
PLUS

Try the best multimedia subscription service for romance readers like you!

Read, Watch and Play.

Experience the easiest way to get the romance content you crave.

Start your **FREE TRIAL** at
www.harlequinplus.com/freetrial.